Me, Nessa Joanne Mulholland  ut of her
hobo collecting. And I can't be After all,
this is my biggest Marilynisr ole life.

Come on, Sugar Kane! My ' to begin.
They hover over the keyboard, w to start up
Word. Almost there...

And how could I not have seen it? I mean, this cruise, Holly hearing my Lorelei line, her always gravitating toward the wrong guys...it really is *Gentlemen Prefer Blondes* all over again. Holly is Dorothy and I'm Lorelei, and being Lorelei, it's up to me to find her the right guy. Like Lorelei says about Dorothy in the film, "She needs someone like I to educate her"! Am I going too fast for you? Sorry. It's simple, really.

It's like this: Holly's greatest attribute is that she's smart and gorgeous; mine is that I've done an awful lot of research (read: watching Marilyn Monroe attract men in film after film); so with my knowledge and Holly's...everything, we really should be able to meet almost every available guy on this boat. Okay, so we might skip the single guy who's having his one hundredth birthday tomorrow, but everyone else, as far as I'm concerned, is fair game. All that I need to do now is teach Holly everything I know about men (and thank goodness for Marilyn, or I'd know nothing). Goodbye intimidation, hello...hmmm... I can't think of the right word. How about: "Goodbye intimidation, hello beating them off with a stick"? Hmmm, that's not bad.

Still, I bite my lip (ouch! I forgot I'd hurt it for a second there) when I think about how this is going to look. I mean, what I'm about to put down on paper (well, computer screen), it's not exactly something the feminist movement would applaud. But it works. I've seen it work. Maybe not in person, but Marilyn certainly pulls it off time after time. And if Holly can pull it off too (and why shouldn't she—she's an A-List actress, just like Marilyn), I guarantee she'll get to know every man on the ship. If she tries what I'm suggesting, no man on earth could possibly be intimidated by her. Then, when she's done attracting them all and has worked out which ones she really likes, she can throw out the dead wood and slowly but surely introduce the stayers to the real Holly. It'll be easy. In fact, she'll probably have too many guys to choose from.

THE LIVING BLOND TRILOGY

Diamonds Are A Teen's Best Friend

The Seven Year Itch

How To Date A Millionaire

DIAMONDS

are a
Teen's
Best Friend

Living Blond 1

by

ALLISON RUSHBY

Diamonds Are A Teen's Best Friend

Contact Information: Allison@allisonrushby.com

First paperback edition November 2013
Cover Art © by Berto Designs. All rights reserved.

Publishing History
First Edition, 2013

Print ISBN: 978-1492969464

Published in the United States of America

DIAMONDS
are a
Teen's
Best Friend

One

"Is this the boat to Europe, France?"

Honestly, I tried to stop myself from asking the question, I truly did. In front of me, the porter guy looks at me as if I'm a thirteen (almost fourteen!)-year-old idiot. Beside me, dear old Dad looks at me as if I'm delusional (that's because a lot of the time he actually thinks I am—he's even had me tested to make sure I'm not). And he's about to open his mouth to start in on me (again...sigh) when, behind me, I hear it—someone laughs. Right on cue.

I swing around quickly, my head zipping from side to side, trying to see who it is, but it's practically impossible in this traffic jam of a crowd, especially when you're as short as I am and your dad won't let you wear a kitten heel, let alone rhinestones in the daytime. I bet Marilyn Monroe's mother never said a thing about Marilyn wearing rhinestones in the daytime. Then again, Marilyn Monroe's mother let her get married at sixteen and spent a great deal of time in a mental institution, so that's probably not saying very much. I'm just about to give up on the searching thing when the crowd parts and someone dressed entirely in red, going out/in/out (in all the right places) and hips swaying, passes me by with a wink and a lift of one perfectly arched eyebrow.

"Honey," she says, in the kind of voice that makes everyone turn and look at her. "France is *in* Europe."

Oh. My. God.

It's one of those moments when you just know you'll think up a zillion and two perfect things to say later, but instead you stand there looking like you've recently had a lobotomy. Especially when I realize that the someone is actually a Someone and that the woman now heading up the escalator to the biggest ship I've ever seen in my life is, in fact, Holly Isles.

Yes, *the* Holly Isles.

Actress. Goddess. Star of stage, screen and various tabloid magazines that you skim as fast as you can at the supermarket checkout because your dad will never let you buy them, Holly Isles.

Someone whistles. And this time, I don't need to look around. This time, I know for sure it's not for me. (Laughing, sure. Whistling? I am sincerely doubting it...) And because I don't turn around, I don't move for the guy. The one who smacks into my shoulder and says, "Excuse me. I need to get to my *aunt*."

I follow his gaze directly up the escalator to Holly. His aunt? Holly is his aunt? Well, la de da. I go to give him my best "Get your filthy mitts off me, don't mess with the outfit and don't go *anywhere* near the hair, buster" look when my mouth drops even further. Hello, sailor! Cute boy ahoy! This guy is definitely related to Holly in a big way.

"Ah..." my dad exhales, the lecture he'd been working on giving me obviously forgotten. Funny, but he's got the same kind of lobotomy look as me. And he's staring straight at Holly.

It takes me a moment to get over the shock. When I finally do, my eyes move back from my dad to Holly's form as she goes up, up, up (and I'm not alone, I think everyone on the dock is watching Holly go up, up, up). Slowly, I shake my head from side to side. I can't believe it. I can't believe Holly Isles just said that to me. And it wasn't exactly the line from the movie I was thinking about, but then again, neither was mine. And I could probably go on watching her forever, my mouth hanging open (okay, so I only check out her nephew a few more times), except that Holly's now out of sight and my dad has obviously returned to his old lecturing form.

"Nessa Joanne Mulholland."

"Mmmm."

"NESSA JOANNE MULHOLLAND!"

"Huh?" I finally look up, only to see him looking down at something. At my chest. Ugh. Gross. What is he doing? He'd better not be doing any research on me. But then I look down too.

Oops. The tissues are escaping again.

I surreptitiously stuff them down my black-with-leopard-skin-trim top with one hand. "I've got a cold, okay?" I mutter. Geez. So much for Marilyn's mother. I bet she never had to put up with this kind of harassment from her father, either. Except that no-one was ever quite sure exactly who he was. And, of course, Marilyn didn't need to stuff, either, did she?

I sigh my second sigh of the morning. Life. It's just so...unmovielike.

Okay, okay, okay, so I guess I should explain the Marilyn thing. And the boat thing. And, well...everything. (Don't ask me to explain the tissue thing, though. We've only just met!)

Right. It's complicated and there's a lot to get through, so listen up, or you'll miss something. I suppose I'll start with the Marilyn thing. Just in case you're beginning to think I'm a bit weird. Here's the deal: I guess you could say I'm a little, um, for want of a better word, *obsessed* with Marilyn Monroe. I have been for quite some time now. And why wouldn't I be? I mean, the woman is, was, *amazing*. I don't know how many movies of hers you've seen, but I've seen them all. Every single one (even the last one, which was never finished). And about a million times. Each. I mean it; I just can't get enough of Marilyn. Why?

I can't exactly explain it, but it's like, when I'm watching her, I can't take my eyes off her. I've heard actors who worked with her say it was like that in real life too—that if she was in the same room as you, later on you wouldn't be able to say who else was there. It was only you. And her.

Lots of people don't understand why I love Marilyn's movies—saying that all she ever did was play the dumb blonde. But they're wrong. *Sooooo* wrong. Marilyn was no dumb blonde, and she didn't play dumb blondes either. If they bothered to look beneath the retina-blinding peroxide hair for a second, they'd see that Marilyn's characters were smart cookies. They got what they wanted every single time and generally five minutes before they knew they even wanted it. Plus, they had a great time along the way.

I really wish I could explain it better. You see, it's not one thing in particular I love about Marilyn, it's just...oh, everything. The hair and the clothes and, most of all, the attitude. She's such a scream. I wish I could get away with saying half the things Marilyn came out with. I mean, that her *characters* got away with, because it's more the movies I'm interested in. The rest of it—the husbands, the drugs, the Kennedys, the on-set trailer tantrums—leaves me a little cold.

Anyway, to cut to the chase, over the years I've come to realize something: Marilyn and I, we actually have quite a lot in common. (No, not the only-person-in-the-room thing. Generally no-one notices if I'm in a room at all.) Like what? Well, for example, our initials—NJM. Norma Jeane Mortenson. That's her. Nessa Joanne Mulholland. That's me. My dad thinks it's a coincidence (especially as it was "Vanessa" before I insisted on "Nessa"). Still, I think it's a sign.

And, where Marilyn is concerned, I see a lot of signs. I call them Marilynisms.

I don't tell my dad about them much anymore. Not since the time when, a few years ago, he sent me to see a special kid psychiatrist. I think he was starting to believe my addiction to all things Marilyn had something to do with my mother's death (she died when I was six). But it doesn't, really. Or at least I don't think it does. I'd never let on, but, if anything, it's probably got something to do with the fact that Dad and I seem to move every five minutes. At least Marilyn's a friend I can take with me. She doesn't even take up a lot of room—plenty of space on my laptop for all her movies!

My dad is a professor who specializes in (wait for it, it's *sooooo* embarrassing...) sociology. What's so embarrassing about that? Well, it's kind of a special type of sociology. Kind of the human mating type of sociology (yes, I know, *ewwwww*). Can you believe it? That's actually his job. Nosey parkering his way into other people's sex lives. Sick, yes? I can only dream of having a dad who's a lawyer. Or an accountant. What I'd give to be able to say that: "My dad, he's an accountant. He works in the city. He commutes in our station wagon." Ha! I wish. Instead, we travel the world, from college to college, landing wherever Dad can get funding to ask his next round of gut-twistingly embarrassing sexual questions of people he's never met before. So far we've lived in Berlin, London, Toronto, Sydney, and now we're leaving New York City. I think we originally come from Australia. At least, that's where I was born and it's where we've lived the longest. It's also where my passport says I come from if you look at the cover. And there's a bit of an accent left in me...somewhere.

Right. That's done. I'll move on to the ship thing then, shall I? All of this brings us to where we are now—boarding the most gigantic ship I've ever seen in my life, the *Majestic*. Once again we're moving on. But this time, at least, is a little different. Dad's using the trip as part of one of his (yes, gut-twistingly embarrassing again) studies. For the last month or so he's been busy interviewing women going on this cruise, and as soon as we set sail, he'll continue watching them. (No, he's not a "Do you want me to apply your sunscreen for you?" pervert; it really is for scientific research.) It's all something to do with whether or not their behavior changes once we're at sea. Something about people thinking cruises are romantic, blah, blah, blah (he tends to give me his proposals to read, but they mostly make my brain either switch off, or my eyes poke out in fright). Seriously. He needs to quit watching and start dating in my opinion. Maybe if he got a girlfriend he wouldn't be quite so interested in what everyone else is doing. Then I could convince him accountancy is a good thing.

Alexa totally agrees with me on the quit-watching-and start-dating point. Who's Alexa? Alexa Milton, my best friend and another Marilynism. Marilyn's third husband was Arthur Miller. Alexa Milton. AM. Arthur Miller. AM. That's no coincidence as far as I'm concerned. NJM and AM. We were meant to be best friends. Fate and all that (though, hopefully we won't get divorced after five years).

Alexa's got a weird life, just like I do. Her parents are archaeologists, and Alexa spends her life being dragged from one dusty dig to another. Still, at least if her parents asked the people they're studying those gut-twistingly embarrassing questions, nobody would be embarrassed at all, because the people they're studying are always dead. That's how Alexa and I met, through our parents (still hanging around college at their age—sad, really). We try to keep them apart because when they get in the same room together they tend to go on and on about how, one day, we'll thank them for our unconventional upbringing. How it will have "expanded our minds." Whatever. At the moment the only thing it's expanding are our typing and texting skills.

Alexa's not so big on the Marilyn thing, but she's watched all the movies with me (the fifth and sixth times I might've had to bribe her with sour cream and chives Pringles), and she gets where I'm coming from. Sort of. Which is good enough for me. At the moment, she's stuck in the middle of a large expanse of red dirt somewhere in Turkey, with no phone reception and only intermittent Internet to keep her sane. I keep telling her I'd swap her any day (parents are far less likely to embarrass you when you're in the middle of nowhere surrounded by dead people), but she hasn't decided whether she'll take me up on my offer yet. She says the cruise sounds great, but having a peeping Tom for a dad leaves her a bit cold (he's really not a pervert, I swear). One thing we do agree on, however, is the fact that being separated over the summer is both cruel and unnecessary, though my dad says it might be cruel, but it's more than necessary. Especially if we want to eat for the next year and have luxuries like electricity.

Phew. I think I got through all that in record time. It may even have been a personal best. (Attending five different schools in eight years has seen me hone the story of Nessa Joanne Mulholland to five minutes or less.)

Anyway, speaking of Alexa, my fingers practically started itching to email her when Holly Isles did her thing as we were boarding the *Majestic*, because it really was like the start of *Gentlemen Prefer Blondes*. You know, when Lorelei and Dorothy are boarding their boat headed for France? No? Okay, I guess you probably don't know. But, believe me, it is. I just couldn't help myself with the "Is this the boat to Europe, France?" line. Just like

Marilyn's line in the movie. And then Dorothy, oops, I mean Holly, lobbed the next line from the movie right back at me. Another Marilynism to add to my collection! Maybe this trip won't be so bad after all. Especially if Holly's fiancé is around somewhere (Kent Sweetman—also super-famous!). Though I wonder where he was this morning? According to all the magazines, they were supposed to be getting married this weekend. So what's she doing on some cruise with her (extremely cute, sorry, I really couldn't help noticing...) nephew?

Hmmm. Weird. Could it possibly be this trip will be semi-interesting?

love it ♥ ↓

Gentlemen Prefer Blondes

Simply the best Marilyn movie ever. Marilyn stars as Lorelei Lee—a savvy, blonde, fun-loving, hip-grinding, rich-husband-and diamond-seeking missile. She and best friend Dorothy Shaw (Jane Russell), a street-smart brunette who won't settle for anything but true love, leave their New York showgirl lives behind them and make their way to Paris on a cruise ship.

Once there, Lorelei hopes to marry rich nerd Gus Esmond, but his father has other plans. Esmond senior plants a private detective on the ship, hoping to catch Lorelei with other men and expose her as a gold-digging schemer. Naturally, guys can't help but be attracted to her, and the private detective soon has a wealth of ammunition (and pictures) that appears to prove Lorelei isn't faithful.

The two girls have to use every ounce of their charm and smarts to get the photos back, prove they're not diamond thieves and get themselves married by the end (Lorelei to Gus; Dorothy to the private detective, of all people). Amazing outfits and the *best* songs, including "Diamonds Are a Girl's Best Friend."

I give it six out of five stars.

TWO

"Nessa Joanne Mulholland."

Oh, how I wish my parents had never given me a middle name. Or a first name. Or even a last name for that matter.

"I thought we agreed we were going to tone it down a bit on this trip?"

Did we? I can't remember. We're always agreeing to tone it down a bit. On this trip. For that party. During this, that, and the other important dinner. Though I've yet to work out just what the old guy means by "tone it down a bit." Could he just mean be me but a bit more quietly? And again, honestly, I did try to hold back. It was only that I'd gotten a bit excited after seeing Holly and having her realize what I was on about with the "Europe, France" line.

And so, when the boat pulled out, I couldn't help myself with the throwing of the streamers and the waving like a weirdo and the "Bye, lover!" line. (I think I may have scared half to death the little wizened-up old wheelchair-bound grandpa who was directly below me on the dock. One of my streamers didn't unroll and fell straight down onto his head, and he then looked straight up at me as the lover thing left my mouth. I waved my hands a bit harder then and yelled out that I didn't mean him, but the boat honked over the top of me, and I think I ended up scaring him even further.) Now, I give Dad my best fluttering of eyelashes, and he shakes his head sadly.

"You know, one day that's going to work on some man, and you won't know what to do."

I go to open my mouth and tell him maybe before that happens I'll read his paper on the subject, when I think better of it and shut it again. Two Marilynisms is pushing my luck already for one Dad day, and looking inside the cabin door that he's just opened in front of us, I really don't want to be spending a lot of time in the sin bin of the high seas. We both go to move into the cabin at the same time and get stuck.

"Umph. Sorry," we say in unison, then laugh.

Dad lets me through first and moves in one step behind me. (That's as far as we both go before hitting the first single bed.)

"Um, there's no window," I say, looking around the room (and, believe me, it doesn't take long). "And what's that noise?" I end up yelling as "that noise" gets louder and louder.

"That would be the engine."

"Oh."

"Sorry?" Dad says.

"OH!"

"Oh," he says, working out what I said in the first place.

Yes. Oh. Something tells me I won't be running into Holly Isles, Kent Sweetman, or the cute nephew down this end of the ship. And by down I mean *down*. Because I've just figured out why there's no window. There's no window because sea level is somewhere a few stories above our heads. This is cruising the college-grant-funded way. And something *else* is telling me the grant won't be running an expense account for all the garish, cocktail umbrella and plastic monkey-festooned mocktails I'd been planning on having.

Sigh.

I turn around to see Dad contemplating the ceiling. When, after a while, he doesn't look down, I decide to have a look too.

"What is it?" I eventually ask when I'm more than sure there's nothing up there worth looking at.

"Ever seen *The Poseidon Adventure*?" He finally returns his head to the upright position.

"No," I say. And for the next ten minutes he fills me in on the glory of the movie *The Poseidon Adventure*. Something about a cruise ship that gets hit by a tidal wave (gee, *thanks* Dad...) and overturns. And the smart people on board decide to try to work their way to the top—really the bottom—of the boat in order to get out through a hole. And just when I'm starting to wonder if there's a moral to this story, Dad contemplates the floor and finishes with:

"Think of it this way—if we overturn in the middle of the night, we won't have far to walk to find the hole."

He's not wrong. There are probably only a few feet between us and that mega-sapphire that what's-her-face stupidly chucked over the side of the boat in *Titanic* (why? WHY?!). "I'll try to remember that," I tell him. "Boat overturns, go up, not down." My dad. Always passing on important and useful life lessons.

"Good girl."

I spend forty-five seconds putting all my stuff away and stowing my bag (when you move as much as we do, you learn to pack light), and another five seconds checking out the bathroom (which gives me time to look it over twice). Then I grab my laptop and stand in position near the door, ready to make a break for it. "Dad..." I whine.

He looks up from his spot on the bed where he's already working through some notes. "Hmmm? Oh, you want to go. Well, that's okay. Just check back in every so often, won't you?"

I nod. And then wait. "Dad..." I start up again.

"Hmmm?" He doesn't look up.

"Daaaaad..."

Now he does. "Oh. Money. I should've known. It's been five minutes at least." He hands me a twenty-dollar bill before giving me the eye. "Make it last, sunshine."

"Thanks, Dad!" I'm off before he can change his mind. Or remember that he never asked for the change from last night's takeout (oh, how I love it when he's in the middle of a study). "Bye, lover!" I yell as I make a break for it.

The lyrical sounds of "Nessa Joanne Mulholland, tone it down a bit" sound up the corridor behind me as I go.

I make my way up to one of the upper decks, where I walk around and generally have a bit of an explore. Talk about gigantic! Not one, but four swimming pools, an aerobics room, a gym, three restaurants...there's even a day spa (not that I'll be seeing the inside of that, but maybe I can convince Dad a bit of a back waxing can sometimes be a good thing for a guy's love life?). It's quiet up here—only a few people are strolling around. I'm guessing the others are still unpacking in their cabins. (I can see how if you were in a suite above sea level, staying in your cabin with your huge balcony, complimentary fruit platter, and bottle of champagne wouldn't be a half-bad idea.) When I'm done looking around, I settle down on a wooden sun lounge, facing out to sea, and spring open Sugar Kane (my precious, goes everywhere with me, pink laptop—named after Marilyn's character in *Some Like It Hot*). I've got to email Alexa.

I'm only a few short sentences in when the drinks waiter (I could live like this all the time!) rolls up. I ask him for some Dom Perignon 1953 (you guessed it—Marilyn's favorite drink), and he gives me a "Why don't you crawl away and die, young whippersnapper" look that makes me wonder how he's going to make it through this trip. I mean, it's only day one. I settle for a mocktail of his choice with not one, but two maraschino cherries (though he'll probably include a chewed-off toenail or three now that I've been smart with him). And there goes well over half of my twenty bucks. Eeekkk. I'd better sharpen my whining skills this trip, or I could easily die of thirst.

Mocktail ordering done, I try to get back into my email, but find I've left my typing fingers on land. I'm completely and utterly distractible—every person who walks past makes me look up, or I find myself simply staring out to sea. I'm way too excited to type. The fact is, I just don't do cool very well. It's fun being somewhere new that isn't another college campus. And with all the Marilynisms that have been going on this morning, I'm finding several movie scenes playing through my head in vivid Technicolor. There's the one from *Gentlemen Prefer Blondes*, for a start. After Lorelei and Dorothy board their ship, Lorelei hangs out on a wooden sun lounge (just like I'm on!) and checks out the eligible guys on the passenger list.

Maybe I should ask that drinks waiter for a passenger list when he comes back? I remember his expression when I asked for the Dom Perignon. Hmmm. Maybe not. And speaking of eligible guys, it's not looking like there are very many at all. The ones who have walked past me so far have either been way grey, too young, or attached to a female. And I'm guessing the Olympic team isn't on board like they were in the film. Pity. I could have done with a whole relay team just for me. It's always been a dream of mine to fall in love with a guy named Skeeter (he was one of the relay team guys)...

Stop it, Nessa. I shake my head. Back to the emailing. Think of poor Alexa, stuck out there in the middle of the technology-Skeeter-and-mocktail-free desert.

"Well, hello there." A figure stops in front of me, casting a shadow over Sugar Kane. I look up.

Oh.

"Mind if I sit down?"

Do I mind if Holly Isles sits down beside me? I think not. "Um, er, sure," I finally manage to stammer, but by then she's already well seated. And I think I smelled her coming before she even arrived. In a good way, I mean. She smells all flowery and citrusy and vanillaery all wrapped up in one. She smells fantastic. How come perfume never smells like that on me? Is there some kind of pheromone they hand out when you turn eighteen? One that makes you a Woman with a capital W?

For something to do (I think my hands may be shaking), I snap Sugar

Kane closed and then take a great interest in the drinks waiter, who's making his way over with my mocktail.

"Wow. That looks pretty good. Living the high life already?" Holly laughs as he puts it down beside me. (He even calls me "madam"! And I notice he's given me *three* maraschino cherries. What a guy...)

"I think I'll have one too," Holly says then. "Maybe a pina colada?"

The drinks waiter nods. "Of course, Miss Isles. Shall I put it on your room?"

"That would be perfect."

Oh, if only he'd known *my* name. Oh, if only I had a *tab*. (Unfortunately my dad isn't that stupid. He didn't get all those degrees for nothing.)

"Do they all come with three cherries?" Holly asks quickly, just as the drinks waiter is about to head off.

"Of course they do, Miss Isles."

She winks at me and *I* laugh.

"Yes, I thought they might." She nods and we both watch the drinks waiter make his way back to the bar. "I love a good maraschino cherry," she says with a sigh and leans back into her chair, closing her eyes.

There's a pause, and as Holly's eyes are closed, I take the opportunity to have a really good look at her. She looks just like she does in all her films. And I can't believe her skin—it's flawless. I can only dream about having skin like that and not having to creep up to the bathroom mirror each morning praying there won't be an eruption somewhere on my face. Plus, what she's wearing—it's amazing. Some kind of a swing coat with a black singlet and black Capri pants underneath. You can tell it cost a fortune just by glancing at it. Frankly, looking at Holly Isles (though I think I may be staring now) is like looking at a car crash: you know you shouldn't, but you can't help but gawk. Of course, five minutes has gone by where I haven't made a complete idiot of myself, so I have to go and wreck this by not being able to help myself again. "Tell me you're from Little Rock," I say a little too fast.

Holly turns her head and opens one eye. "Sorry. Dayton, Ohio. It was worth a try, though."

"I guess."

"You're a bit of a Marilyn fan, are you?"

She knew! She knew what I meant about "Little Rock"! I try not to look too excited. "You could say that." I take a sip of my mocktail. "Want to try?" I offer Holly the glass.

"No, it's okay. I'll wait for the stronger stuff. After the week I've had, I need it."

"Oh." I don't know what to say. Should I ask where Kent is, or not? I'm not sure on the star etiquette thing. "Um, do you want to talk about it?" I try.

Holly sighs. "I'm sure you don't want to hear it."

Get real! Of course I want to hear it! Still, I try not to look like a gossip hound. "I don't mind. I'm a good listener. I have to listen to my dad all the time." Holly laughs at this. "No, I mean, he's always telling me about his studies and stuff."

"Studies?"

"Mmmm." I take another sip of mocktail. "He sort of studies, um...people."

Holly's eyebrows raise a bit. "People? What do you mean? Is he a journalist?" she asks quickly.

I shake my head just as quickly back. "I wish! It's nothing as glamorous as that." Oh, no. How did I get myself into this situation...again? "He sort of studies people and how they, um...mate." I mumble the last bit.

"What? You're joking." Holly sits up in her chair.

"Really?"

"Yes. Really. He's a sociologist." I can't believe I just told Holly Isles my dad's a sex fiend.

"Wow. He'd have a field day with Kent then." She sits back again.

That's probably true, I think to myself, if even half of what I've read about him in the tabloids is correct. Suddenly I find myself looking at my mocktail intently. I poke around in the glass a bit with my straw (especially when I find a lump that I really, really hope isn't a piece of toenail). The pause is longer this time. Much longer. Finally, I look up. "So, did you want to?"

"Want to what?" Holly looks over at me, confused.

"Talk about it."

"Oh. Right. Um..." She gives me a look. One that I don't really like because I can tell, in that assessing moment as her eyes skim over me, that she suddenly realizes I'm a kid. Thus, I'm safe. She can tell me anything.

"Hey, if you don't want to..." I start, and Holly waves a hand.

"No, it's not that." She gives me one last, thoughtful look. "It's just that there's not much to talk about, I'm afraid. It's all said and done. The wedding's off."

Holy...I try not to jump out of my sun lounge. Not much to talk about? I can think of a few gossip columnists who would disagree. "Oh, really?"

Silence.

I'm not quite sure what to say now, but eventually it comes down to two choices: to ask or not to ask. Being me, I opt for ask. "Was there, um, someone else?"

Holly snorts. "Several someone elses, it seems. Including our pool cleaner. That was the someone I caught him with."

Ah. Er. What do I say to this one? And why is she telling me all of this? Isn't it a bit of a secret? "I'm..." I shrug. "I'm sorry to hear that."

And Holly must see the look in my eyes because she snorts again. "It's okay. The pool cleaner was a woman. And why am I telling you all of this?"

I have no idea. "Maybe you need to let it all out?"

Holly snorts. "Maybe. Anyway, it's not okay, is it? About the pool cleaner, I mean. But good riddance, I say. My grandmother never liked him anyway. I should have listened to her. She always said that any man who changed his name from Kenneth Mananopolous to Kent Sweetman couldn't possibly be any good, and it turns out she was right. Plus, it's not like he was much..." She trails off as she turns her head to look at me. And I think she must suddenly remember my age again, because she changes tack fast. "I mean he wasn't much...of a mocktail maker."

Hmmm. Sure. I eyeball her. "I do know people have sex. I'm, um, sixteen, you know." Sixteen? Where did that come from?

Holly laughs. "Oh, yes. I forgot about your dad."

"*I* didn't." I roll my eyes like the true sixteen-year-old that I now (sort of think I) am. There's another pause.

I use it to develop a more worldly voice. "It's a bit sad, though. That you broke up."

Holly looks away quickly. "Well, it's not like it hasn't happened before."

Ouch. I think back and remember the Kent thing had always been a bit off and on. And from my tabloid study I know Holly's been engaged at least twice before. Hey...my head whips around as I see something out of the corner of my eye. It's a guy. A tall skinny guy about halfway down the deck. A guy with a camera. And he's taking photos of us. I open my mouth to say something to Holly, but then he turns and starts taking photos of other people. Oh. I shake my head. Duh—he's the ship's photographer. For a moment there I thought he was spying on Holly or something. I'll have to remember to go and look at the display of photos later. And I'll have to buy a million copies to send to everyone I've ever known!

Beside me, Holly sighs, still looking out to sea. "Yes. On the man front, I seem to be setting a trend."

Huh? Oh. Oops. How bad do I feel now? Holly's telling me all about her two-timing fiancé, the guy she was ready to spend the rest of her life with, and I'm sitting here wondering how many photos I'll be able to badger my dad into paying for. "Maybe you're just a hobo collector?" I say the first thing that comes into my head (always a mistake). This was something Lorelei had said about Dorothy. She always picked the wrong guy too.

"A what?"

"A hobo collector. You know, always picking the wrong guy. It's like my Aunt Greta. My dad's sister. She collects meantiques."

"Meantiques?" Now Holly really looks at me.

"Yeah. Too-old men who are mean to her."

Holly practically falls out of her chair, she laughs so hard. "You're a scream, you know that?"

I'm not sure what to say, so I just shrug and polish off my mocktail. "Want a cherry while you're waiting?" I offer Holly my glass. She smiles at me as she reaches over to pluck one out.

"Only if you think you can spare one."

My heart has stopped beating.

I think I am going to die of happiness.

Holly and I lounge for a good few hours, shooting the breeze and another mocktail (for me; Long Island iced tea for her) or two. Of course, we keep ordering extra maraschino cherries (eventually the drinks waiter just brings us a bowl of the things). And Holly must need someone to confide in desperately, because I hear it all. Her perfectly lined and filled red lips fill *me* in on her sad and sorry love life, right from guy A to guy Z.

"And now," she says, finishing off her life story with a flourish of one hand, here she is on what would have been her honeymoon cruise, with her nephew, of all people, to keep her company.

Speak of the devil. Just as the word "nephew" exits Holly's mouth, up he stalks.

"I was wondering where you'd gone," he says, standing over Holly's chair.

Holly grins up at him (I think the pina colada and Long Island iced tea might be working their magic on her now). "I love you too, Marc, sweetheart."

I can't help but giggle at this. Whoops. Marc turns and shoots daggers at me.

"And you are?"

"Oh, Marc. Lighten up. This is Nessa. My new best friend. We've been having a lovely girlie chat."

"So I see." Marc eyes the glasses lined up on the table beside us.

Pray, scat, I think to myself, as I throw him what I hope is a haughty look. That's what Marilyn would have done (except she would've had the guts to say the "Pray, scat" thing out loud, like her character Lorelei did in *Gentlemen Prefer Blondes*). As for "new best friend", I can't even think about that now. My brain will explode.

Marc turns his shoulder then, effectively blocking me out of the conversation. "There's a call for you," he says to Holly. "There have been *several* calls for you."

Hmmm, interesting, I think as I look up at his broad back (also pretty yummy).

Holly sighs now and leans forward to look at me beyond Marc's legs. "That's my cue. Better be off before I get in trouble."

"Sure," I say. "Thanks for the second mocktail, Holly. It was fun."

"No, thank *you* for letting me vent. And it's not just everyone who'd give you one of their maraschino cherries, you know."

"No worries!"

"I'll see you around." She gives me a quick wave as Marc drags her away by one arm.

Party pooper.

As Holly leaves, I watch her curves and high heels and swing coat go with a shake of my head. I can't believe I feel sorry for her. Holly Isles. I never would have imagined someone like her would be so desperate to talk to somebody that she'd talk to me. She obviously needs some help, stat, as they say on all the medical shows. And she also needs to amputate that dour (but still, I have to admit it, awfully cute) nephew as well. Preferably before he turns gangrenous. (Green, black and purple, especially when seen on the extremities whilst cruising, is so out this season...)

three

FROM: "NJM" <toohottohandle@mymail.com>
TO: "Alexa Milton" <alexainexile@mymail.com>
SUBJECT: I am such an idiot!

Alexa! Where are you when I need you? (Don't answer that, I already know...) Now, sorry to butt in on your misery, but you'll never believe who I just met—Holly Isles! (Scream here.) Yes. Holly Isles! (Scream again here.) And you'll never believe who I never properly introduced myself to— Holly Isles! (Restorative slap here.) Yes. Holly Isles! (Restorative slap again here.)

Ugh. I am such an idiot. I let Holly Isles sit beside me for ages (will fill you in later as have to rush off—important cruise ship business to attend to, you know) and I never told her my whole name (which means she couldn't call my cabin for another chat, even if she wanted). We talked for ages, too. She even called me her "new best friend"! Can you believe it? I can't. I really can't. I'm Holly Isles's "new best friend." I'm starting to wonder if I didn't hit my head on some metal railing and dream up the whole thing (more likely, I'm sure you'll agree). Really got to go. Will tell all later, I promise, promise, promise.

Nessaxxx

My fingers fly across the keyboard as I type my quickie email. I've got to go. It's almost four and dinner starts at eight, which leaves me with half an hour to attend to my "important cruise ship business", and three-and-a-half hours to get ready (and it might just take that long to get my eyebrows into some kind of shape).

The thing is, when I got back to the cabin after my chat with Holly, my dad had surprised me with the news that we were going to be dining at the proper restaurant tonight. As in, not slumming it at the buffet. Tonight, we'd be at the adults' table! Of course, the first thing I did was check the time. Quarter to four? Was he kidding? And now, five minutes later, he must see the look on my face.

"What's the matter, pumpkin?"

This, at least, makes me pause. I look at the floor. At the beds. At the tiny writing table. "I don't see any ground-dwelling vegetables here, Father."

"Yes, yes. I remember. I won't call you 'pumpkin'. But what's up? You've got something to wear. We bought you something special. Remember?"

I forget all about being Holly Isles's "new best friend" and bite my lip, shifty-eyed, because I suddenly remember he hasn't yet seen how I altered the "something special" number that made me look five years old. Uh oh. "Of course I remember! It's just that a girl needs time to get ready..." (Remember the eyebrows? I wasn't joking about that). Anyway, no time to think about this. I turn toward the door, blowing a kiss at Dad. "Must fly, dahling."

"Dahling? Fly?" The poor guy looks totally confused. His natural state, I've come to realize.

I turn back for one second. Just long enough to roll my eyes at him. "Do you think I'm just naturally beautiful? No. It takes work. Work and *people*." Oh, how I wish I had *people*. I'm sure Marilyn had people. And plenty of them.

He's still rating a 9.75 on the confusion scale.

"It's okay, Dad." I reach over and pat him on the arm (sadly, I can do this from my position in the doorway).

"It'll all be okay. Really it will."

"Hmmm. So much for 'toning it down'. Nessa, I'm not sure what you're talking about, but 'people' sounds expensive. Just don't a) spend a lot of money or b) fall overboard, and I'll be a happy man."

My hand still on his arm, I pause, wondering whether he really meant to place his requests in that exact order. Still, I think I can manage to toe the party line on this one. "Well, I'll try to cut back. I won't have the caviar face mask after all." I give his arm one last pat, wink, and close the door behind me.

And, for the second time today, "Nessa Joanne Mulholland!" follows me up the corridor.

I already feel right at home.

m

"Here's the thing..." I look up at the *maitre d'* and put on my best doe-eyes. Then, at length, I fill him in on "the thing." The thing being the fact that I want to try to weasel my way onto Holly Isles's table for dinner. Well, me and my dad's way. I work my magic on the French guy with the little twiddly moustache standing in front of me to the best of my abilities. But my so-called abilities must be quite poor, because after I'm done, there's a pause...and then he laughs.

Laughs long and hard.

"This is a joke, yes?"

I stare at him. Maybe I got the doe-eyed thing wrong? I give up, let it go, and try fluttering my eyelashes instead.

"Little girl, the head waiter is making you come here and say this? It is one of his, how do you say it, practical jokes?"

Little girl? Head waiter? Practical joke? What?

I flutter harder. I am sophisticated. I am classy. I am a *young woman* who knows what she wants (not even close to being a "little girl").

"Little girl, what is wrong with your eye? Is there something in it? Are you about to have a fit?"

I stop fluttering and start to panic slightly. Now what?

In front of me, the *maitre d'* folds his arms. "Tell me. How much does he give you? I will double it if you go back and tell him I have put you on the table."

"You're going to put me on the table?!" Yes! I can't believe my luck. How easy was that? "Thanks!"

His eyes roll back in his head, his breath sucks in, and now, he guffaws. "Of course, I am not going to put you on the table! Are you crazy?" He pronounces this "crazee." "Everyone wants to be on Mademoiselle Isles's table. And some of them are even willing to pay."

Oh. Right. Now I get it. I should have remembered. I'd seen Marilyn seek out the *maitre d'* in one of her movies when she wanted someone seated at her table for dinner. Everyone wanted to sit on Marilyn's table too (and had been willing to pay for the pleasure). She'd ended up threatening to take all her meals in her room if the *maitre d'* didn't do what she wanted.

Which meant that he'd have to give all the money back that he'd taken from people.

Hmmm. Somehow I don't think that's going to work for me. I'm doubting the *maitre d'* would care if I stayed in my cabin for the rest of the trip, sucking on a single dry cracker for sustenance. I dig around in my pocket, hoping there's magically going to be a hundred dollars in there. There's not. But there is a ten. "How about if I give you this?" I hand it over to him.

He laughs again, looking at my outstretched hand. "You are crazy, little girl."

I stuff the ten dollars back in my pocket. Fast. "I am *not* crazee. And I am not a little girl!" I scowl my best scowl (and it's much better than my best doe-eyed look, or my eyelash fluttering).

He stops laughing when I say this. "Now I am really not going to seat you on Holly Isles's table."

No. I'm guessing he's not. I turn around and start the long trudge toward the elevator, the thick carpet making my feet feel heavier with every step. When I finally get there, I reach out and press the button to go down. Down, down, down to the depths of the ship again. Well, at least my physical depth will match the depth of my misery. Why did I think this would be so easy? I'm no Marilyn Monroe. I'm no little girl, either, but when I look down and see my jeans and T-shirt, I realize I'm not exactly sophisticated and classy, like I'd thought before.

Ugh. I don't even want to go to the dinner anymore. For a start, my dad's going to flip when he sees what I've done to my dress. He is *not* going to be a happy pappy. Looking at my reflection in the shiny elevator doors, my shoulders slump even further. Like I have a choice in the matter. I'm going to this dinner tonight and that's that. Well, maybe I'll at least get to talk to Holly tonight. And I'll probably get to see that nephew of hers in a tux. That should be worth leaving the cabin for...

Where is this stupid elevator? I reach out and press the button again. And again, and again, and again. Then I cross my arms, feeling the *maitre d's* eyes on my back. He's probably still having a good laugh at me, I think, waves of embarrassment flowing over me. How dumb was I? Thinking that I could just waltz in and do a bit of table bargaining, Marilyn style. I mean, what did I have to bargain with? Ten bucks. Ten bucks I'd got off my dad. Well, whoopee. Ugh. No, double ugh. Hurry up, hurry up, hurry up...I want to reach out and kick those buffed-up doors. I'm sure I can feel his eyes on me. *Don't look, Nessa. Don't look.*

So, of course, I look.

And I'm right. The *maitre d'* waves at me. "Enjoy your treep!" he says smugly.

I give him my best withering look (and it's pretty good—I'm a teenager, after all). And I think I'm done when I turn back around and choke half to death. Marc is standing right in front of me, the elevator doors now wide open.

He looks almost as surprised to see me as I am to see him.

"Er, hi," he says gruffly. "Nessa, isn't it?"

I nod dumbly. He really is good-looking. No, scratch that, he's *great-looking*, I think to myself as he runs one hand through his hair.

"Er..." He looks to one side of me.

Oh, no. He wants to get out. "Sorry, sorry," I say and step aside, then realize I'm waiting for the elevator myself and step back again so I can get in. Which means that Marc and I collide. Hard.

"Oopphh", I think, is the not very ladylike noise that escapes my lips as our shoulders collide. And I'm just about to lose my footing and end up on the floor when Marc grabs me by both arms, pressing me into him and squeezing the air out of my lungs. He hugs me for a second or two until I'm standing upright again. Though it feels like two minutes. Maybe even three. When I'm finally balanced again, he pulls back.

"Sorry. You okay?" His expression has completely changed. When he looked at me before, it was as if I was smelly road-kill on the highway of life. Behind him, the elevator doors slowly close again.

"Um..." I start. Am I okay? I'm not sure. I'm actually feeling kind of dazed, though I'm not sure if that's from our little accident, or being pressed into Marc's chest. (I really should fall over more often.)

"Nessa! You're bleeding." He steps forward now and touches my lip, bringing his finger back to show me a spot of blood.

I'm bleeding? I *am* bleeding, I realize when I see his finger. I reach up and touch my lip as well. I must have bitten it when we collided.

"Mr. Harris. Mr. Harris, you are all right?"

Huh? I turn around to see the *maitre d'* closing in on me. Who's Mr. Harris?

"Mr. Harris?" He's looking straight at Marc. Oh. Duh. Marc is "Mr. Harris." Still half dazed, I watch as Marc steps to one side, so he's standing in front of the *maitre d'*. And there it is. That look again. The road-kill look. But this time, it's not directed toward me.

"I'm fine," he says. "It's Nessa who's hurt."

I shake my head now, waking up to myself. "It's okay. I'm okay." I wave my hands.

"No, it's not okay," Marc continues, glancing over at me for a second before turning back to the *maitre d'*. "You saw what happened. You heard me say Nessa had hurt herself. So why are you asking me if *I'm* all right?"

"I, er, I..." The *maitre d'* doesn't quite know where to look.

I reach forward and press the elevator button again. Please, oh, please let it come faster this time. "Ha ha," I laugh nervously as I step back once more. "I'm fine. Really I am. Just fine." I touch my finger to my lip again and it comes away clean. "See?" I hold it out. "No blood. Just fine."

"That's not the point." Marc's still staring down the *maitre d'*.

Suddenly, thankfully, the elevator appears. I squeeze into it as the doors are still opening and start pressing the "close doors" button immediately. But the doors keep opening, and opening. And Marc and the *maitre d'* are both looking, and looking. Oh, man. I press the button a few more times and, finally, the doors start to close. "Yep, just fine. Um, thanks." I don't look at Marc, but his feet. Thanks? Thanks for what? The doors have almost closed now. "I'll see you around." I finally bring my eyes up to meet his, which look like he doesn't entirely understand what's just gone on. And the last word or two I say to the back of the elevator doors.

See you around? Nice work, Nessa.

Ugh. How embarrassing. I hope I *don't* see him around. Maybe not being able to swap tables was for the best after all.

Four

I take a deep breath and open up the bathroom door. "Ta da!" I say, hoping the flourish of my arms will distract my dad's attention away from my dress. I've done a few small alterations on it when he wasn't looking. Like taking the original high-neck, long-sleeve top off the full pleated skirt, and replacing it with this cool vintage Marilyn-style white halter-neck number found in a recycled clothes shop in Chelsea. (There have been definite shopping advantages to our recent six-month stay in NYC. Ones that, frankly, never presented themselves during a short-lived, three-month study stint in Laos.) I've given myself loose curls as well. It's really easy—you do them around empty single-serve Coke cans. Though drinking all that Coke can make you rather gassy, and drinking all those tiny single-serve Cokes from the mini bar can lead to instant death (not from the Coke, from your parental figure when they see the bill).

Anyway, the outfit's all very *Seven Year Itch*. You know, the scene where Marilyn's skirt blows up? That one.

I'm also hoping to distract my dad's beady eyes away from the eyeliner and beauty spot I've got on. (I get away with mascara, a bit of blush and lip gloss, but Dad tends to freak when I take things any further. In his mind, I'm eternally piggy-tailed and five years old. Daddy's little girl...)

Except that it's not the dress or the eyeliner, as it turns out, but something else entirely that distracts him. Sitting on one of the single beds, his eyes suddenly look watery.

"You look more like your mother every day."

Oh.

He sucks in his breath then. "Sorry, sweetheart. You look lovely. Just lovely." He smiles a fake smile.

I turn around and take another look at myself in the mirror. A good hard look. But I can't see my mother at all. I try hard to match my features up with hers. All the ones I've seen in the photo albums. Because that's all I have, really: photos. A few vague memories of her voice, and photos. Sometimes I'll think I remember something we did together—a trip to the park, to the zoo, baking a cake—but then I'll see a photo of us doing the same thing and realize I've somehow worked the photo into a recollection. Sometimes I wonder if I truly remember her at all.

Dad once said that the best way I could remember her would be to convince everyone I meet to become an organ donor. Because that's why she died, you see. She had cardiomyopathy. A virus you get in your heart. And she might still be alive today if she'd had a heart transplant. But there weren't enough hearts to go around. There never are, apparently. So, as soon as I get my driver's license, I'm ticking that "Do you want to be an organ donor?" box. Both my dad and I are on a list too, somewhere. Some kind of organ donor registry. When I turned thirteen we had a big talk about it— about whether I wanted to be a donor or not. There wasn't much to talk about, though. I figure I won't be needing my heart after I die. And if someone else can use it, well, they're more than welcome to it. As I keep looking at my white-outfitted reflection in the mirror, searching for my mother, I remember something else—something I'd heard my dad and the kid psychiatrist talk about outside his office. (Of course I listened at the door, wouldn't you?) The psychiatrist had said something about my making up a fantasy world based around Marilyn Monroe because my real world was so transient. My mother had gone and we moved so often—the world in my head couldn't be taken away from me as easily as the real world seemingly could. I've never really known what to think about that...

Dad gets up off the bed and comes over to turn me around and give me a kiss on one cheek. "You do look lovely," he says, smiling down at me. But then the smile fades. Oh, no, I think. He's really upset. He's going to cry.

Wrong.

Instead, the smile fades to a sharp narrowing of the eyes. "Nessa Joanne Mulholland. That's not the dress I bought you, is it?"

Just when I thought I'd got away with it.

There's another look. And a licking of a thumb that quickly makes its way toward my face. "Now, come here. You've got a smudge on your cheek."

Aaaggghhh! Incoming Dad spit!

m

I try really, really hard to look sophisticated and accustomed to walking in heels as we exit the elevator (another Chelsea bargain that Dad didn't know about until five minutes ago). I've even resorted to using a bit of double-sided tape, nicked from a passing steward, between the bottom of each shoe and the soles of my feet. (Not very Marilyn, I know, but needs must...) And heads do turn on our arrival, but they also turn back again very quickly when they see we're not Someones. Oh, well. Someone who doesn't turn away, though, is the *maitre d'*. I can tell something's up the moment I see him and he fixes me with a "Not very happy, young lady" look as Dad and I cross the floor (me hanging on to his arm for dear life to keep from tripping and falling inelegantly on my face).

"*Bon soir*, Mademoiselle Mulholland," the *maitre d'* says through his teeth when we reach his small desk. "A pleasure. Yet again."

"You've met?" Dad looks at me, and I shrug slightly, my face frozen. I'll get the lecture of the century if he finds out what I've been up to (trying to get us seated on Holly's table, that is). Let's just say that my dad...he isn't keen on celebrities. He thinks anyone who lives on the West Coast (especially within a million-mile radius of Hollywood) has to be a bit dim. Beauties can't have brains in my dad's little universe. Anyway, he may not be keen on celebrities, but I hope he *is* keen on sitting next to either the kitchen or the bathrooms. Because that's where I'm thinking we'll be sitting tonight.

The *maitre d'* glances at the list in front of him, before lifting his head once more to really give me a look. Something *is* up, I think to myself. Either that or the guy's going to pass a kidney stone in about thirty seconds. "Well, it looks like you will be on table three tonight." The eyes narrow. "Enjoy." He practically spits the word. "James..." He clicks his fingers and a guy materializes from behind one of the potted palms. "Show Professor and Mademoiselle Mulholland to their table, please. Table three."

James looks at us, then pauses, as if he can't quite believe what he's hearing. "Table three?"

The *maitre d'* whips around then. "Yes, table *three*. That is what I said, is it not?"

James gives us the once-over again. "Table three. This way, please."

Table three. I'm half scared to follow him. Because I'm starting to think that table three is the one in the middle of the fancy fish tank. The one with the miniature sharks in it.

But, as it turns out, that's not where table three is at all. And it's nowhere near the kitchen or the bathrooms, either.

Table three is Holly's table. The best table in the room. And I can hardly believe my eyes as James guides us over to it. How did this happen? Had the *maitre d'* felt bad and seated us here after the lip incident?

When we get close, Holly sees me and waves, and Marc half-turns in his seat. I wave at Holly and smile at Marc, who doesn't smile back. Hmmm. Busted lip or not, it looks like I'm back in the bad books again.

"Who's that?" My dad squints, seeing me wave at Holly.

I sigh as I look up at him. "You shouldn't have to ask."

"Oh. Do I know her? Is she from the college?"

Now I really sigh. Is she from the college? It's like he really *is* from a different universe (more specifically, planet college, in the clueless system). "No, Dad. That's Holly Isles. The actress."

There's a blank look.

"Come on, Dad. Even you must know who Holly Isles is." I pause for a second, turn him to face me, and count down her three biggest and latest films on three of my fingers.

"Ah. I think I have it," he nods slowly, when I'm done. "Didn't they film part of that last one at the college?"

Aaaggghhh! Why can't I have a normal father? One who lines up to see all the blockbuster films with a supersize bucket of popcorn and a giant Coke instead of taking an apple to the art house cinema? Yes, that's right. An apple. To the art house cinema. On date night.

"Don't you remember? We saw her boarding the ship this morning."

Another squint.

"Come on, Dad, you definitely saw her. I saw you seeing her." I remember his lobotomy look that matched mine all too well.

There's a third squint. "Oh! Oh, yes I do remember now. She's very beautiful." And a pointed look. "Though I did no such thing." Then he looks back at Holly again and there's a long pause in which I can practically hear his brain ticking over. Wait for it, wait for it..."But how do you know her?"

I knew it! The man may be from the clueless system, but he zaps back down to earth from time to time to keep an eye on me. I know we'll have to get this all sorted and out of the way before we take one step further. It's a Dad thing.

"Um, I met her before. On one of the top decks."

The look changes from confusion to "What have you been up to, Nessa Joanne Mulholland?" fast. "I hope you haven't been bothering people."

"*Moi*?" I'm all innocence. "Of course not. Now, come on. And do try to tone it down a bit, won't you..."

"Looking gorgeous, Nessa." Holly stands up and gives me a kiss first on one cheek and then on the other (how LA!) when we finally reach table three. "Love the outfit."

"Thanks! I love yours too." And I do. What I'd give to be able to wear a strapless number like that. Holly's long black and white shimmering sequined dress is mesmerizing.

"And this charming gentleman must be your father?"

I nod and do my introductions. First to Holly, then to Marc. "You'll have to come and sit next to me," Holly says to my dad. "Nessa's told me all about your work. It sounds fascinating. And I haven't sat beside a professor for years. Actually, I think I only ever sat in front of them, so this is a first for me."

"You went to college?" My dad looks surprised, and I surreptitiously kick him on one ankle. He is *such* a snob! Like I said, Dad and celebrities don't mix. Just because Holly's an actress he assumes she's stupid.

Holly nods. "Microbiology was my poison. Nothing nearly as interesting as sociology, I'm afraid."

"But microbiology's a fascinating field." My dad, animated now, reaches out and touches Holly's arm. "Only the other day..."

And this is where my brain switches off. Holly and Dad sit down beside each other and, amazingly, start nattering away like they're old friends. As for me, I take a seat beside Marc, who's chatting to the man sitting next to him...and continues chatting to him through a bread roll (I eat Dad's as well, for something to do), salad, and the appetizer.

Looks like Holly's got a new "new best friend."

It isn't until our main meals begin to arrive and Marc's friend ducks off to the bathroom that he turns to me. Grudgingly. "I hope your lip's okay," he says gruffly, not really looking at me. The waiter places my plate in front of me—an extremely yummy-looking chicken breast stuffed with macadamia and coriander, sitting on some sort of mango sauce. (I could do this every night! Way better than Dad's develop-your-cellulite-while-you're-young repertoire of lasagna, sausages, and pork chops.)

"It's fine, really. It looked a lot worse than it was."

Silence. Except for on the other side of me where my dad cackles loudly. I look at Marc. "Holly must be bored out of her mind."

I'm expecting him to agree with me when he shakes his head and takes a mouthful of his lamb shank. "No," he says when he finishes chewing. "I don't think so."

I pause. "How do you know?"

"Er..." Marc pauses as well, his fork halfway to his mouth.

"What? What is it?"

"Er, nothing." He takes another hasty mouthful.

I wait for a moment before I decide I've had enough. Who does this guy think he is? One minute he's sticking up for me, the next minute I'm no-one. "Look. You've been ignoring me all evening. You may as well tell me what you think. How do you know Holly isn't bored?"

Marc finally meets my eyes. "Fine. Okay. I know because she'd send me the signal if she was bored."

Now I really pause. "The signal?"

Marc looks cagey. As if he shouldn't be telling me this.

"We have a 'save me' signal. You know, for the weirdos and the freaks who don't look like weirdos and freaks initially. Sometimes it's hard to tell. Anyway, Holly can signal me, and I'll know to come and rescue her."

"Oh. So, what's the signal?"

Marc's busy buttering another roll. "Well, I can't tell you that. She might want to use it on you." He laughs slightly at this.

Complete and utter silence follows his comment. Marc continues buttering until, mid-buttering stroke, he realizes what he's just said, freezes, and looks over at me. "Sorry, Nessa, that was an awful thing to say. I didn't mean..."

I almost want to cry. I'd thought Holly and I had had such a great time together earlier today. I thought...

"Nessa." Marc reaches out and touches my arm. "It was just a joke. Holly's not going to use any signal on you, believe me. She was raving about you all afternoon."

I perk up a bit on hearing this. "Raving? About me?"

Marc laughs. "Yes, you. She thinks you're quite a character for a sixteen-year-old. That's why I was coming to see the *maitre d'*. To see if he knew who you were. Holly wanted you at her table for dinner."

So that's how...hang on. Holly Isles wanted *me* at her table? Me? My brain takes a while to register what Marc's just said.

"You don't need to look so surprised."

"But I am surprised." Not including the fact that I'm surprised everyone's buying the sixteen-year-old thing.

"What? No-one's ever wanted to sit with you before?"

Now I laugh. "Maybe it's happened once or twice in the school cafeteria, but it hasn't happened with an Oscar-winning actress before, that's for sure."

Marc shrugs. "That's not all she is..." And there's that gruff tone again. I watch as he returns to his roll.

"You're pretty protective of her," I say slowly, watching him.

Marc pauses, sizes me up, and then nods. "Everyone around Holly's protective of her. Sometimes I wonder who's looking after who, really. I guess we're both looking out for each other. And, look, I'm sorry if I seemed a bit into myself this afternoon, and just now, but you have to be careful. Holly's very...*trusting*, I guess, is the word. She lets people into her life too easily sometimes, and certain types of people take advantage of that."

"Well, I'm not trying to."

He sighs. "I know. I know. It's just hard to tell sometimes. And when it happens, I get so angry. Like the *maitre d'* this afternoon. I mean, he didn't care that you'd hurt yourself. And he wouldn't have cared if I had either, except he knows I'm traveling with Holly Isles."

Now there's a question I've been meaning to ask. I place my knife and fork down on my plate so I can give Marc my full attention (and this is saying something—the chicken really is good). "So why are you traveling with Holly?" I ask. And then the conversation really starts.

As we finish off our mains and move on to dessert, then on to a scrumptious cheese platter, Marc fills me in on, well, Marc. As it turns out, we've actually got quite a lot in common. Marc comes from a family pretty much like Alexa's and mine—nomadic. His parents are surgeons who've spent the past two years working for *Médecins sans Frontières*. (That's "Doctors Without Borders" to non-French-speaking plebeians like me.) According to the latest letter he's had from his folks, they've been traveling to Sri Lanka and are hiding out on an island just north of their destination, trying to avoid a particular Tamil Sea Tiger stealth boat. So far they've been searched twice and all their supplies have been confiscated by the army. (My eyes grow wider and wider as Marc tells me about their adventures—it doesn't exactly sound like Club Med.) While his parents have been dodging bullets overseas, Marc's been living with Holly in order to finish high school (unlike me, the lucky thing's got less than a year to go).

"That must be weird," I butt in then.

"What's that?" Marc stabs a piece of blue cheese.

"Living with Holly."

"Well, not really. She's my aunt. Always has been. Even when she wasn't Holly Isles, if you know what I mean."

I nod. "I guess. Don't you miss your parents?" Talk about the most uncool question that's ever left my lips. I must remember to introduce my brain to my mouth sometime this century.

But Marc doesn't seem to think so. He looks straight at me when I ask this. "I worry about them. A lot. They weren't going to go until I started college, but they were needed. They're both amazing surgeons. They can really help the organization out. I talked them into it in the end."

I bet he did. I would too, given half the chance. But then I look over at my dad and change my mind. He wouldn't last five minutes being chased by a Tamil Sea Tiger stealth boat. He'd probably try to win the rebel fighters around by inviting them over for afternoon tea and a chat about something sad like the theory of evolution. (That's the oh-so-exciting topic he's raving on about at the moment with Holly, who, amazingly, still hasn't sent "the signal." Maybe she's forgotten it?)

"And Holly talked me into being here," Marc continues.

"On the cruise?"

Marc nods. "It was supposed to be her honeymoon. Her and Kent's. The first thing we had to do on boarding was move into a suite with two bedrooms and two normal beds."

Two bedrooms? I can only dream. "Oh."

"The honeymoon suite only had a gigantic four-poster."

Ugh. I make a face.

"My thoughts exactly."

I glance over at Holly for a second. Sitting beside my dad, she looks happy, like she doesn't have a care in the world. She really is a good actress. "It must be awful for her. Is she very upset?"

Marc glances at Holly as well. "She's good at hiding it. After the last few times..."

I nod.

"If she hides her feelings, the magazines make less of it, and it's easier for her, I suppose."

I just don't understand it, I think to myself, shaking my head as I stare at my plate. Maybe if I'd met her and she'd been a complete cow. If she hadn't been like she seemed in all her films and interviews—the happy-go-lucky girl always willing to sign an autograph and talk to her fans.

"What is it?" Marc asks.

"Why?" I look at him, puzzled.

"Why what?"

"Sorry, I mean why do they always dump her? She's so nice. I can't believe anyone would dump Holly."

Marc snorts. "It's always the same reason. Always. The guys—they're such losers. They're intimidated by her. By her success. Kent's the perfect example. A couple of his films flop, hers don't, and he's off. They just can't bear it. It's pathetic, really."

I think back to her last fiancé—Tom Hollings. And to the one before that—Jude Johnson. Maybe Marc's right. Tom had tried to move from being a sitcom star to a film star and failed miserably. Jude had ended up directing a film that ran way over budget and was still a real turkey.

"What she needs is a guy who isn't in the industry at all. A guy who isn't even interested in it. But she never meets anyone who *isn't* in the industry."

"Oh, come on..."

Marc leans forward. "No, it's true. Have you been to Hollywood? LA, even?"

I shake my head.

"Well, it's really like that. It's like living in a different universe. And the industry's everything—you can't get away from it. If Holly grabs a coffee, the barista will try to get her agent's number. If she hires a new cleaning lady, she'll leave a film script on the toilet cistern in the hope that Holly will read it. It's weird. I've been trying to convince her to move to her place in New York, but she's still umming and ahhing about it."

"Wow." I can hardly believe what Marc's just told me. "Is that really true, about the cleaning lady?"

He nods. "And that's not all. The last time Holly's clothes came back from the drycleaners, there was a film script packed into the bottom of one of the bags with a note begging her to read it."

"Weird."

"Definitely. Anyway, like I said, if she's got any hope of having a lasting relationship, she needs to meet different kinds of men. All sorts of men. That's why I ended up saying yes to the cruise. I thought she should get away from LA. Even if it's just for a bit. France isn't really far enough, but it's a start. And she wouldn't go without me. So here I am."

I laugh at the idea of France not really being far enough away and, beside me, my dad turns around. "Having a good time, pumpkin?"

I give him the "Do I look like an orange vegetable in my exquisite get-up?" face. And he must be having a really good time with Holly, because he's Mr. Playful. He reaches out and pinches my cheek. "You'll always be my little pumpkin."

Oh, great.

Next to him, Holly laughs, her own cheeks pink. She looks like she's been having at least a half-good evening.

"You're lucky to have such a great dad, Nessa."

Mmm. Right.

"You ready to go, sweetheart? I've got two interviews tonight and an early start tomorrow."

I nod, even though I don't really want to go.

Holly sighs. "I didn't even get a chance to talk to you. I meant to pop down to your cabin this afternoon and give you something for your lip. I've got this cream—it works miracles on bruises, it really does. How about I come down tomorrow morning?"

I think about our cabin. I don't think there's room for a third life form in there. Not even a mosquito. "How about if I come up?"

Holly nods. "Sure. That would be great. Should we say 11 a.m.? We're in 1256."

After we say goodbye to Holly and Marc, Dad and I both turn, link arms, and start the long, stumbly walk back to the bottom of the boat. (High heels—who invented them?) We pause outside for a moment in the cool, salty-smelling sea air, lean on the railing and look out to sea.

"Holly's lovely, isn't she?" my dad says, after a while.

"For an actress?" I shoot him a look.

"I never said that."

Hmmm.

"This afternoon, when you came back to the cabin, you didn't tell me you'd met her."

I hadn't had a chance. And then later I'd been racing around like a mad thing trying to get ready for this evening, hassling the *maitre d'*, bumping into people and making myself bleed, putting single-serve Coke cans in my hair, and drawing on fake moles. You know, that kind of thing. Girl stuff.

"You must really like her," he says. Dad then takes my arm again, and I wobble across the deck to the stairs that lead down to the next set of stairs that leads down to the next set of stairs that leads down to our cabin.

I look up at him. "I do. But why?"

"Well, she said you gave up one of your maraschino cherries."

"And?" I'm not getting him.

"One of your maraschino cherries? I should be so lucky!"

This makes me laugh. As he starts down the first stair, I stop and plant a kiss on his right cheek. Mwah. "Dad, I'd give you one of my maraschino cherries any day, and you know it."

He looks smug. "Well, yes. I thought as much. But I wanted to hear it from the horse's mouth."

Five

It comes to me in the middle of the night. With the ship's engine going full steam ahead next to my left eardrum, I sit straight up in bed. That's it! All through my shower, getting changed, crawling into bed (literally—this room is so small, I don't have much choice) and trying (unsuccessfully) to fall asleep, Marc's words about Holly had reverberated in my mind—mainly that Holly is always getting dumped because men are intimidated by her. That Holly needs to meet different kinds of men. All sorts of men. That she needs a guy who isn't in the industry. But now, now I've got it. I know how I can help Holly out. I know what I have to do.

But first...I turn my head and check on Dad. Not that I really need to—he's snoring. In time with the engine, no less. Excellent. Quietly, quickly, I reach over and grab my jeans, a T-shirt, woolen wrap (that's the nice way of saying "down-market pashmina"—I don't think I could be trusted with the real deal) and my green flip-flops, and get changed out of my pajamas. Then, again quietly, quickly, I locate Sugar Kane and tiptoe out of the cabin, slowly, slowly opening and closing the door behind me.

Then I stop and wait on the other side. What I'm waiting for is my dad to bounce out of bed and spring the door open with an "Aha!"

Waiting, waiting...Phew. Looks like I'm okay.

I head up to the deck where I'd been with Holly earlier today and sit in the chair she'd cocktailed and maraschino-cherried in, for inspiration. I look around me as Sugar Kane starts up. There's absolutely no-one about. Not a great surprise, as it's 1.30 a.m. and more than a bit chilly. But I've got better things to think about than being cold. I know how I can help Holly out. How I can help her to attract a different sort of guy. How I can get her out of her rut.

Me, Nessa Joanne Mulholland, I'm going to help Holly Isles out of her hobo collecting. And I can't believe I didn't think of it before. After all, this is my biggest Marilynism yet. The biggest one of my whole life.

Come on, Sugar Kane! My fingers are dancing around, ready to begin. They hover over the keyboard, waiting. Finally. I press the button to start up Word. Almost there...

And how could I not have seen it? I mean, this cruise, Holly hearing my Lorelei line, her always gravitating toward the wrong guys...it really is *Gentlemen Prefer Blondes* all over again. Holly is Dorothy and I'm Lorelei, and being Lorelei, it's up to me to find her the right guy. Like Lorelei says about Dorothy in the film, "She needs someone like I to educate her"! Am I going too fast for you? Sorry. It's simple, really.

It's like this: Holly's greatest attribute is that she's smart and gorgeous; mine is that I've done an awful lot of research (read: watching Marilyn Monroe attract men in film after film); so with my knowledge and Holly's...everything, we really should be able to meet almost every available guy on this boat. Okay, so we might skip the single guy who's having his one hundredth birthday tomorrow, but everyone else, as far as I'm concerned, is fair game. All that I need to do now is teach Holly everything I know about men (and thank goodness for Marilyn, or I'd know nothing). Goodbye intimidation, hello...hmmm... I can't think of the right word. How about: "Goodbye intimidation, hello beating them off with a stick"? Hmmm, that's not bad.

Still, I bite my lip (ouch! I forgot I'd hurt it for a second there) when I think about how this is going to look. I mean, what I'm about to put down on paper (well, computer screen), it's not exactly something the feminist movement would applaud. But it works. I've seen it work. Maybe not in person, but Marilyn certainly pulls it off time after time. And if Holly can pull it off too (and why shouldn't she—she's an A-List actress, just like Marilyn), I guarantee she'll get to know every man on the ship. If she tries what I'm suggesting, no man on earth could possibly be intimidated by her. Then, when she's done attracting them all and has worked out which ones she really likes, she can throw out the dead wood and slowly but surely introduce the stayers to the real Holly. It'll be easy. In fact, she'll probably have too many guys to choose from.

Yes. It's the plan of the century. Foolproof. But to put it into action, Holly will need to study, and study hard. And thankfully, now Word's loaded, I can get on with her first lesson—Lesson I. (Everything looks more scholarly and important when you use Roman numerals, you know.)

NESSA'S LESSONS IN LOVE

Lesson I: Femininity is the key

At all times, be feminine. Men love a woman who pampers herself. Long baths with sweet-smelling vanilla oil are good (this will remind him of Mother's home cooking—and you don't have to let on, that despite your brand-new gourmet kitchen, you've never cooked anything more than a microwave dinner in it). Manicures and pedicures are good. Facials are good. Time spent on hair and make-up is good. However, when complimented, you should never, ever show that you have gone to any trouble. As for clothes, short and tight is *not* what you are looking for. Remember: *femininity* is the key. Shapely calves and ankles should definitely be displayed. A hint of bronzer-enhanced cleavage is also good, but don't overdo anything.

Lesson II: Flirt

Play with and toss your hair, smile, look up at him through your eyelashes, take his arm, stroke his lovely suit material (the material you just complimented). Keep it light, keep it bubbly, keep it giggly. *Never* get serious.

Lesson III: Act helpless

Men like to be good at the "boy stuff." Let him drive (and read the map), let him fix your TV/alarm clock/zipper. Let him order for you, open doors, pull out chairs, and help you across the road as if these things would never happen if it weren't for him.

Lesson IV: Let him have all the answers

Never monopolize the conversation. He knows everything and you know...well, not nothing, but not very much. If he starts to tell you about how fascinating iguanas are, and you happen to have done your thesis on the species, don't let on. Simply gaze at him attentively. The iguanas won't let on.

Lesson V: Be unavailable

It's never good to look like no-one wants you, so pretend

you've got a boyfriend even if you don't have one. Even better, pretend you've got quite a few. This means a) plenty of guys want you; and b) that you flit lightly in and out of situations and he'll think that he'll be able to flit lightly in and out of your life too. Remember at all times that you need to attract as many men as possible. (Think of moths to a lit candle, flies to a bug zapper...) This means they'll have to compete for your attention, and they will—it's always good to be the alpha male.

Right. I think that's it.

I sit back in my chair and puff my cheeks out, only feeling the cold again because I've stopped concentrating so hard. At least my fingers are warm. I bring my hand up to my face to warm my cheeks, checking my watch as I go. Three a.m.?! I snap Sugar Kane shut and jump up. I've really got to get some sleep. After all, today's going to be a big day. I've got to convince Holly that a little bit of love study is in order. And something tells me that's not going to be easy.

"You're kidding, right?" Holly looks up from the piece of paper I've given her and laughs. Laughs long and hard. And yes, it's the "Nessa's Lessons in Love" piece of paper I'm talking about here. And hang on, let me go back and rephrase that...Holly looks up from her sumptuous cream silk-padded bay window seat, silhouetted against her stunning, endless sea view. Oh, and that's in her *private* lounge room. (Marc has one of his own, which is a good thing because I'm not sure he'd exactly approve of the Nessa's Lessons in Love message if he was here.)

"Tell me this is where the cameras come out. Nessa, sweetheart, you can't actually believe this." She holds the paper out in front of her, pinched between two fingers as if it's got some kind of disease.

I go over from my spot in the middle of the (cream plush-pile-carpeted) room. I retreated there after I gave her the missive so I could see her reaction, and I guessed it would be something like this. Now for the convincing. "I knew you'd say that," are the words that come out of my mouth with a sigh.

"Are you really surprised? This is advice from the dark ages!" She brings the paper in again to read aloud from it. "Keep it giggly. Never get serious. Gaze at him attentively. Shapely calves and ankles should definitely be displayed...Nessa, I'm ashamed of you!"

Wow. I guess this really *is* going to take some convincing. Maybe even more than I thought. I walk over to sit down beside Holly in the bay window seat (adopt me, please).

She shakes her head as she reads over the lessons once more. "How could I follow any of this? I'd look like a complete bimbo."

"Aha!" I'm quick to jump in here with a waggle of one finger. "But that's the point, isn't it? It's all about the bimbo. The bimbo always gets the guy!"

Holly looks up.

"Well, she does, doesn't she?" I say.

"I don't think that's a good thing."

"Aha!" I jump in again. "That's true. But only for *us*. It suits the bimbo just fine though, doesn't it? The thing is, we've learned that being a bimbo is bad. But is it really? Maybe it's fun. Who knows if you never try it?"

Holly keeps on looking at me.

"It's not like bimbos ever hurt anyone, do they? So they look a little dumb, but so what? It's just flirting, and all flirting really is is making other people feel good about themselves. It's about being interested in *them*. In really listening to them and what they're saying, rather than thinking about what you're going to say next."

Silence. And then, across from me, Holly's brow crinkles thoughtfully. In a "Huh, that's funny, I never thought about it that way before" kind of way.

Excellent. I'm making progress. But, um, er, now what? Maybe I should try to explain it another way. Really hit the message home. In the continuing silence, I gather my thoughts until I come up with something. "Look. I don't mean to be rude, but whatever you've been doing for the past number of years, it's not working for you, is it?"

Sitting across from me, Holly's eyebrows raise a tad.

"So maybe you should try something else for a change and see how it fits?"

Silence. Again.

"But..." Holly looks confused when she finally speaks.

"But what?"

"Well, even if I thought this was a good idea—which I don't—it's not me, is it? I know I'm no genius, but I'm not stupid. I'm not a bimbo. What if I act like a complete bimbo and then I meet someone I really like? What do I do then? I've pretended to be something I'm not."

"No, no, no. That's not how it works. It's only for the initial attraction. The point is to attract as many guys as possible, filter out the ones you're not interested in, pluck out the A-grade ones, and then slowly but surely start showing the real you."

Even more silence.

"Holly?" I try eventually.

"Um, I don't know. It seems kind of silly..."

I go for the clincher. "How many times have you been engaged?"

Holly looks down at the lessons again. "Three," she mumbles. She reads over the entire sheet of paper once more before she looks up at me. "You know what this reminds me of?"

I shake my head.

"Something one of my girlfriends did a few years back. It was called "The Relationship Game." She gave me the book when she was done with it. I thought it was the stupidest thing I'd ever read. All about how you shouldn't call him back for a certain amount of time after a date, so you don't look too desperate. Things like that. I think I threw it across the room in the end."

"Oh." I'm not quite sure what to say to this. But then I think of something. "What happened to your friend?"

Holly's eyes look straight into mine. "She got married six months later. She's just had a baby. And she's blissfully happy."

"Oh."

"Yes. Oh."

There's a pause. A long pause.

"You really think this will work?" Holly finally speaks, shaking the piece of paper.

I think of Marilyn and I nod. Hard.

She takes a deep breath. "Maybe I should humor you, even if it's just for a few hours. If it worked for my friend, it could work for me, too, right?"

Holly's eyes look as if she doesn't truly believe this statement, but I nod again, harder this time, encouraging her.

Holly sighs, watching me. "You know, you put up a pretty good argument for someone so young."

I scoot over closer to her, animated now. "Well, I don't read all my dad's essays for nothing."

Holly nods slowly, all the time biting her bottom lip.

"What's up?"

She frowns. "I'm sorry I dumped all my problems on you yesterday, Nessa. It wasn't fair. I guess I'm just a bit..."

"Lonely?" I finish the sentence for her.

Holly pauses for a second and then shrugs.

"Don't worry about it. Now, listen up, because I've got a few ideas..."

As I sit there and fill her in, my excitement rises. I can't believe I'm thirteen (almost fourteen) and I'm on board a cruise ship. Sitting beside Holly Isles. Giving her advice about love. It's not like real life at all. It's like something that would happen in a movie. Just as I'm thinking this, strangely, I catch sight of our reflections in the mirror opposite us.

And for just a fraction of a second, I don't see Nessa and Holly. I see Lorelei and Dorothy. Marilyn and Jane.

six

Okay. So, over the next few days, I feel like I'm more Skipper to Holly's Barbie, than Lorelei to Holly's Dorothy, but that's all right. I'm sure people feel like that around Holly all the time. You see, I find out very quickly that the terrible thing about Holly is that she's just so awfully, awfully pretty. Not 7.30 p.m. "I've had the whole day to get myself together, so now we can go out on the town" pretty, but "I can wake up in the middle of the night with a raging dose of the flu, vomit, wind up with chunks of carrot left over from dinner in my hair and still be pretty" kind of pretty. And the even more terrible thing is, you can't hate her for it. You can't hate her for it because she's one of those people who doesn't get it at all. Holly has no idea she's this stunningly gorgeous person who's just lovely to be around twenty-four hours a day.

That's the best thing about her—she's simply *Holly*. Not Holly the film star on the red carpet, not Holly dating all the most scrumptious guys in Hollywood, not Holly on the front of every magazine. Just Holly. A chick whose favorite food in the world is nachos (with extra sour cream), who cries like a fool when watching *Pretty Woman,* and who has to paint this icky stuff on her nails so she won't bite them all the time. When you get to know her she's surprisingly...well, real.

Not to mention really, really unhappy. I feel so sorry for her (me, feeling sorry for Holly Isles—a week ago I would have had a good laugh at this one), having to call off her wedding and everything. How awful would that be? To make matters worse, she truly thought she'd found the right guy this time. She says she knew they were having problems, but kept pushing those thoughts to the back of her mind because she wanted everything to be perfect. She wanted, with all her heart, to have found the perfect man. "PM", she calls him. Perfect Man. And they'd have the perfect wedding and buy the perfect house and have the most perfect babies. But as it turned out, she didn't have the perfect man. He wasn't even close. Obviously, she didn't have the perfect pool cleaner either. (Strangely enough, she seemed more than a little upset about the pool cleaner. Apparently it's hard to find a good one in LA.)

I listen to Holly's tale of woe over and over again. Sometimes she cries about it, sometimes she throws pillows and magazines at the wall about it, sometimes she tries to reason it all out. And as I listen, it only cements further in my mind what I already know: I've been put on this ship for a reason. It's no coincidence that I know everything there is to know about Marilyn Monroe and that Holly belted out her Dorothy line in reply to my Lorelei line as we were boarding the ship. We were meant to meet because Holly needs me. So I've got a job to do here. I have to help Holly out. I have got to help her find the right guy. There won't be any more broken engagements. No more heartbreak. Holly deserves to find PM this time around, and I'm going to find him for her.

Here's hoping he's on this ship.

But no. Of course he is. Why else would fate bring us together and then not plant the perfect guy on the ship? Yes. He's definitely here, no doubt about it. Now, all we've got to do is meet every guy on board in order to flush him out. Right. So how are we going to do that?

FROM: "NJM" <toohottohandle@mymail.com>
TO: "Alexa Milton" <alexainexile@mymail.com>
SUBJECT: Brain on holiday

Help! My brain's seen the quoits deck and swim-up bar and thinks it's on vacation! I'm supposed to be trying to figure out ways for Holly to meet every eligible guy on the ship, so she can finally meet PM (Perfect Man), fall in perfect love, have the perfect wedding, and pop out perfect babies, but I'm coming up with...nothing. Any ideas?

Nessaxxx

I finish typing my email, press send, then log off and snap Sugar Kane shut with a *click*. That done, I continue lying on my stomach on my bed for a good half-hour, coming up with...again, nothing. In the end, I decide it's just not going to happen this afternoon and drag myself up off the bed. I brush my hair, put on a bit of lip gloss and head up and out onto the top deck of the ship for a stroll. Maybe the sea air will help me think a bit better. (Nothing could help me think worse, that's for sure.)

Up on the top deck, it's quite windy, and because of this, not many people are around. The hard core are still out in force—power-walking around the track, their little hand weights helping to work off that third pancake they had at breakfast. (Meanwhile, their stomachs are thinking about what time morning tea ends and lunch starts. Not that there's anything wrong with that. My stomach's discovered untapped sources of greed this trip as well.) There are a few other people braving the weather along with the power-walkers, escaping from one thing or another, and a few couples scattered near the bow, enjoying the peace and quiet, looking out to sea.

I go to take a turn around the deck myself when I see him peeking around from a pile of deckchairs, not too far in front of me. The ship's photographer. The tall skinny guy who'd taken the photo of Holly and me on our respective sun lounges the other day, which I totally forgot to go and check out. Thinking I've missed out, I race up to him and practically bowl him over.

"Hey!" I say, from behind. And I guess he's not expecting anyone, because he's startled and hits his head on a metal railing behind him. "Oh, sorry! Are you okay?"

"Yeah, yeah, I'm fine." He's looking at me warily, as if I was the one who hurt him and not the railing. He rubs his head with one hand and clutches his camera to him with the other, as if I may reach out and grab it at any moment, then run off, never to be seen again.

Calm down! I think to myself. I don't want your camera. Better tell him why I'm here. "Um, those photos you took of Holly and me the other day. I meant to come and have a look at them."

In front of me, his shaggy eyebrows raise, making him look kind of startled again. Silence. He takes a step back.

"Um...hey, don't hit your head again," I say, pointing above him.

He winces and ducks a little. Weird.

"Um..." I start again, but don't really know what to say. What is it with this guy? "So, did they turn out? Where are they? I mean, on what deck? And how much do they cost?"

Silence again. But, this time, the guy fills the pause by giving me a complete once-over. "Who...who are you?" He shakes his head when he's done.

What? This guy really *is* weird. For a start, he's not making any sense. Who am I? What's that supposed to mean? Oh...hang on. The other day. Holly and I had left before he could take our details. Of course he knows who Holly is, but me? Probably not. I don't have a very red-carpet life. "Sorry, I'm Nessa Mulholland. Cabin 252b. I guess it must be hard being the ship's photographer. I mean, trying to remember who's who and everything."

"Huh?" The guy keeps looking at me, but then he brightens up. "Oh, right. Now I remember. You were the girl with Holly Isles the other day, weren't you?" He whips a notebook out of his back pocket and I can see other names and dates jotted down in there. "Sorry about the mix-up. I didn't get your name. What did you say it was again?"

This time, I spell it out for him. And when that's done, he stops being weird altogether, loosens up, and we even chat for a bit about what I'm doing on board the ship, my dad's study, and how I got to know Holly. When he asks me about Holly's broken engagement and cancelled wedding plans, however, I feel a bit uncomfortable. "I don't know if I'm supposed to talk about that," I say, my eyes not meeting his face.

He shakes his hands. "No, no. I shouldn't have asked. None of my business, but everyone on staff loves Holly so much...we just want the best for her, you know."

Now I do meet his eyes. "Yeah, I know. So how much are the photos?"

Strangely, he looks a bit blank again, as if he can't remember his own prices. "Er, because of the mix-up, how about I slip a couple underneath your cabin door, free of charge?"

I pause. "Really? Are you sure?"

He nods. Hard. "Of course. I hate it when I don't get people's names right. It'd be my pleasure."

"Well, thanks. That'd be fantastic. It's 252b, um..." I realize I don't know the guy's name.

"Ted. Just call me Ted. And don't worry—I've got it all down here," he adds, patting his notebook.

"Great. I'd better let you get back to it, I guess."

Ted nods.

"See ya! Watch out for those railings!" I turn and leave him, walking around the pile of deckchairs and continuing along the edge of the deck. And I'm tripping along merrily when I stop dead in my tracks. Well, hello...look at what's at nine o'clock. I take a few steps back now, out of their line of vision and just watch.

Watch Holly and my dad, that is.

Like last night, they seem to be having an absolute ball together. My dad says something, Holly replies, Dad says something else, and then her head tips back and she laughs and laughs and laughs. When she recovers, he says something else again and she laughs once more. I almost want to rub my eyes. How funny can sociology or microbiology be? And besides all that, I don't quite know what to do now. Do I go over? Do I leave them alone? After all, they seem to be having a pretty good time without me. My dad—I don't think I've seen him look so happy since...gosh, I can't even remember. Oh. Right. Since Jessica, maybe?

My heart sinks when I remember her. Jessica. She was a woman my dad dated for a while. I didn't really like her all that much. Well, no, that's not exactly true. Jessica was okay. It just hadn't worked out. They'd both broken it off, really. Yes. Jessica was okay, but she was no...well, she was no Holly. My eyes lift up as I think this and I take a second look at my dad. And Holly.

Oh, no. No.

I hope my dad doesn't think that Holly being nice to him means the same thing that Jessica being nice to him meant. I mean, Jessica and Holly...they're kind of different people. Jessica was a psychologist. A normal-looking, normal person with a normal job (so she had a few quirks, but don't we all have a few quirks?). But Holly—Holly's in a different league. I keep watching them, laughing and talking, talking and laughing, and my heart sinks even further.

No. This is not good. Not good at all.

Don't get me wrong, it's not that I think Holly's too good for my dad because she's so pretty, or because she's famous, or anything like that. It's just that...well, how on earth would it ever work out? I mean, my dad and Holly Isles. She lives in LA, we're going to live in Paris (well, for a year, at least). She's a world-famous actress, he's a professor of sociology. She dates famous actors, he dates...rarely. Get my drift? Their two worlds—they just couldn't merge and...

"Hey, Nessa! How's it going?"

I whip around on the spot. Marc. Marc is walking up the deck toward me. Oh, no. No. What do I do? I start to freak out and then wonder why I'm freaking out at all. What have I got to freak out about? I haven't done anything wrong. For once.

"Hey, yourself!" I wave back at him and then realize instantly what the problem is: I don't want him to see Holly and my dad. I don't know why, I just don't. So, I race up to him, grab his arm, and spin him around. "Let's go for a walk!" I say brightly. Too brightly, I think. "Not on this deck, though, it's too windy. Or maybe we can catch a movie, or something? Yes. A movie would be great. Any movie. I don't care. We could get popcorn and everything."

Marc gives me a strange look (I don't blame him) and his head twists back for a second, as if he realizes I'm trying to divert his attention away from whatever's up ahead. Don't see them, I chant in my head, don't see them, don't see them, don't see them, don't see them, don't see them. But it's no good. He's looking so far back around his shoulder now that he *must* see them. And just when I'm getting ready for him to say something, his head twists back and his eyes meet mine before he shrugs.

"I saw a movie this morning, but a walk would be great. As big as this boat is, it's making me feel cooped up."

"Great!" I say, still too brightly. But inside my head I think, That's funny, I was sure he'd seen Holly and my dad just then. Positive, even. If he has, though, Marc doesn't say anything. He doesn't say anything about it at all.

FROM: "Alexa Milton" <alexainexile@mymail.com>
TO: "NJM" <toohottohandle@mymail.com>
SUBJECT: What? What?!

Let me get this straight. You are Holly Isles's new best friend, and you are helping her find a new guy? Um, Nessa Joanne Mulholland (to quote your dad), if even 1 percent of any of what you have told me turns out to be true, I will bury myself alive with all the other dead dusties out here. Email me back. Right now. I need details!

Alexa( )( )( )

FROM: "Alexa Milton" <alexainexile@mymail.com>
TO: "NJM" <toohottohandle@mymail.com>
SUBJECT: I'm waiting!

Hello? Anyone out there? It's been 48 hours. It's cruel to keep me waiting. Cruel!

Bad best friend.

Bad best friend.

Alexa( )( )( )

m

FROM: "NJM" <toohottohandle@mymail.com>
TO: "Alexa Milton" <alexainexile@mymail.com>
SUBJECT: Details

Hey! I can't believe your mother let you use the super-expensive satellite phone to call me (the bad influence in your life), even if it was only for five minutes. She must've known you were desperate. That you'd die if you didn't find out what was going on. And you were right—it was an "emergency situation," and that's what the phone's for, after all.

Completely justified.

Okay. So I guess I should fill you in on what's been happening since we spoke. It's been, what, twelve hours? I can't believe it's only been twelve hours. You know something, Alexa? A lot can happen in twelve hours on a cruise ship. A lot, lot more than can happen on dry land, let me tell you. And especially to a thirteen-year-old! It's all a bit manic, cruising. Like any emotion you have is doubled. No wonder Dad's doing a study on it. I still haven't come up with any kind of a grand plan to get Holly to meet every guy on the ship, but that doesn't seem like a huge problem at the moment, because she's doing pretty well on her own. Every time she walks in a room, she gets surrounded by a new group of men. And so far, there seem to be a few likely contenders for PM. She went to a champagne supper with some big shot IT guy last night, a dawn helicopter joy-flight with a tennis player this morning, and then had breakfast with a race car driver. I hadn't heard of the other two, but I know the race car driver's name (Antonio something unpronounceable and Italian). He must be really famous, because even my dad had heard of him (and that, as you know, is saying something).

Speaking of Dad, I feel a bit sorry for him, actually. He and Holly had been having some lovely little chats (like I told you about), but he invited her to have dinner with us last night and she couldn't make it—she's booked up for ages. (I guess you have to get in quick with those Hollywood stars.) She said she'd try to get out of it, but Dad wouldn't hear of her cancelling anything for his sake. Oh! Oh! I almost forgot. She wants to be part of his study. Can you believe it? Holly Isles in one of my dad's creepy studies. I hope the press never gets a hold of any of the details. Can't you just see the headline? It'd be something like: "Holly Isles's saucy at-sea sex life." Shudder. I hope she knows what she's in for.

As for the other thing you wanted—"frequent Marc updates" (what's that supposed to mean, anyway?)—I don't have much else to report there. Yes, we've been spending most of our time together, but we're just friends. Really. That's all. No, really, Alexa. I can hear you making noises from the other side of the world. What else can I tell you? We just get along really, really well. He's a great guy. And that's it. Really. I mean it, Alexa! Stop it!

Anyway, must run. I've got to try to come up with something so Holly can meet all these males floating around with us.

Nessaxxx

I change position on my bed, sitting up and crossing my legs, read back over my email quickly for mistakes, then press send. As it zips away, I think over what I've just said, especially the bit about Holly agreeing to be part of Dad's study. Ugh. I hadn't spoken to Alexa about it, but it's not good that Holly's interested in signing up. The thing is, my dad, of course, doesn't know all about the Nessa's Lessons in Love stuff. (And I can't say I've told Alexa the whole truth about what's going on—I'm sure she wouldn't approve either. In fact, sometimes I think Alexa and I might've been swapped at birth. She's much more like my dad than I'll ever be.)

Over the past couple of days, Holly's been pretty good with her lessons, actually. She's been laying it on thick—batting her eyelashes (three coats of mascara every morning seems to have helped, rather than just one or two), reaching out to touch arms gently as she makes a point (one that agrees with his, of course), and wearing flirty, short skirts. And thankfully, she seems to be having a ball. She says it's been fun. Like being "in character." And she's been getting a ton of dates. So I guess Nessa's Lessons in Love are working after all.

But, anyway, to get back to Dad and his study, I definitely do *not* want Holly being involved. Holly taking on the "lessons" means that I'm affecting her behavior, which, in turn, means I'm affecting Dad's study and his results. Like I said, not good. Not good at all. I'll be grounded forever if he finds out I've affected his results. So, I have to try to get Holly uninterested in the study. I guess if I come up with something brilliant on the meeting men front, then maybe she won't have time for the study. Not a bad idea, really—it'd be killing two birds with one stone, wouldn't it?

The answer comes at lunch. Dad and I are going for seconds at the buffet (cruising, as it turns out, truly is bad news for the waistline), when I see it.

"Nessa! You're holding everyone up." My dad gives me a nudge from behind, moving me on from the rice salad to the Greek salad.

Oops. I've obviously been reading the notice for too long and now everyone in the queue behind us is starving to death. I keep moving along the salads, but at every opportunity, my eyes move back to the notice. "Talent quest", it says, in big letters. "Tonight. 7.30 p.m.. Theme: Hollywood glamour."

I have to keep reading it to check it's true. But it is true. So, today, I don't go back for thirds. Instead, I run off to track down Holly. First, I need to talk her into doing this (which I think is going to take some very creative coaxing). Then we need a routine, dresses, some practice, and some more practice. All before 7.30 p.m..

I finally locate Holly on one of the upper decks, playing badminton of all things. At first, I don't see her. Instead, I hear her giggle. From three decks below. And then, slowly but surely, I work my way up until the giggles get closer and closer.

And there she is...wearing a tiny little pleated white skirt, a white v-neck sleeveless T-shirt and white baseball cap, surrounded by a group of muscly, cruise-wear-attired male admirers.

"Oops!" She throws the shuttlecock into the air and then misses it with her racquet by a mile. (She misses, but her moves, mind you, manage to show off her tanned thighs perfectly.)

But hang on. Walking across the deck toward her, I stop in my tracks.

I've seen Holly play badminton before. She personally whipped my butt at the game just the other day (and I'm not a bad little badminton player, if I do say so myself). Afterward, I'd practically had to stop her doing a victory lap of the deck as well. That girl likes to win.

"Oops!" She misses again now, but flashes her waist this time. Giggle, giggle, giggle.

"Need some help?" The muscliest of the muscle men steps forward (sans shirt) and moves in behind Holly. He reaches around her back, hugging her into him, then lifts up her arms, shuttlecock and racquet still in place, and guides her through the moves. "Like this..." he says as, together, they throw the shuttlecock into the air and then follow through with the racquet.

"Ooohhh, thanks Glen!" Holly pirouettes to face him and then leans into his chest to balance herself. "Oops! Sorry! I guess I'm just little Miss Clumsy today! Maybe I'll need your help for the whole game!"

Ugh. Yuk. My eyes boggle now. What is she *doing*? Why is she throwing the game like this? The guys all move in now. "Can I get you a drink, Holly?"; "Do you need to sit down, Holly?"; "Here, I'll take the racquet for you, Holly"...blah, blah, blah.

And that's when I get it.

Oh.

Well, duh, Nessa.

She's doing exactly what I told her to do. What I'm seeing here—it's Nessa's Lessons in Love in action. And boy is it working, I think as I watch the guys crowd in even further. I'd just been taken aback for a minute there. Watching Holly pretend not to know how to play badminton when she's actually so good at it—it was weird. Kind of disturbing. And, um, maybe not such a great idea after all.

"Water?" I turn my attention back to her as she places a hand on another guy's arm now. "You're too kind. That would be lovely. Just make it Evian. With lots of ice and a squeeze of lemon. Thank you, darling."

Across the deck, I snort to myself. If I tried that line on the guy who's now sprinting off to find Holly her extra-special water with a squeeze of lemon (can't wait for those slow drinks waiters), he'd probably point me to a tap and walk away. That's if he didn't ignore me in the first place, walking over my parched and dehydrated dying body on the deck.

Maybe Holly hears me snort, I don't know, but she sees me then. "Nessa, honey, sweetheart, you just have to come over here right now and meet these perfect gentlemen. They've been teaching me how to play the most amusing game. What's it called again? I can't seem to remember..."

"Badminton!" they chime in unison, their eyes moving from Holly to me for only a nano-second.

Badminton, huh? Oh, brother...

seven

So I was wrong about a couple of things. I didn't need to coax Holly creatively at all. In fact, she said she felt very "devil may care" (whatever that means, I'll have to look it up sometime) and agreed to the talent quest on the spot. The other thing I was wrong about was the practice-and-some-more-practice thing. We actually needed some practice, some more practice, and a whole lot more practice after that. Well, not Holly (who is a natural and picked up the moves and the song in about five minutes flat when she was away from her admirers, had re-installed her brain, and was back to being her smart old self again), but me. Let's just say I wasn't meant for a life on the stage.

When I have to sing (and I don't even sound that great in the shower) and dance (Fred Astaire, where are you when I need some pointers?) at the same time, I don't have two left feet, but three. Maybe even four. I keep tripping up, or getting my timing wrong and bumping into Holly. Instead of getting mad, though, like some people would, she just laughs and tells me not to give up my day job. I explain that'd be pretty easy—I don't even *have* a day job.

By 7.15 p.m., Holly and I are in her suite, staring at ourselves in her mirror. It's a completely surreal experience for me—staring at myself standing beside Holly Isles. In some ways, it's like I know two Hollys: Hollywood Holly (the one everyone knows and sees in her movies and in the tabloids, etc., the one I used to think I knew) and the real Holly (the one who can't control herself around a plate of nachos). Anyway, sometimes, like right now, these two people mesh into one and it gets kind of confusing.

"Hello?! Nessa? Is that you under there, Nessa?"

I wake up to myself to see Holly is laughing at me, looking at my reflection, then over at the real me (or what's left of the real me, anyway).

"Huh? Oh, I'm, um, not sure." I check out my reflection as well. Pink satin strapless dress (thankfully long enough to hide the sneakers I'm wearing—there's no way I could dance in heels—remember the other night? I couldn't even walk across the floor of the restaurant), platinum-blonde wig—can you believe they hire out fancy dress costumes and wigs on board a cruise ship? Holly and I couldn't—a face full of make-up (and I mean *full*—false eyelashes and all), and a diamond necklace, and bracelet of Holly's. I have to keep touching them to check they're both still there and I haven't lost them. Who knew diamonds could be so scary?

"If your dad sees you, he will *kill* me." Holly shakes her head. "You look about twenty-one."

"Really?!" I check out my reflection again. I guess I do look a lot older. It's the make-up. And the...um...the "chicken fillets", as Holly calls them. "You think the chicken fillets look real?"

Our two sets of eyes both move down to my chest, where, underneath my strapless boned gown, two pieces of skin-colored plastic are hiding. Kind of like implants, but on the outside. Holly calls them her "secret weapons"—she doesn't believe in the kind of implants that go on the inside.

"Let's put it this way," she shrugs, "do you think mine are real?"

Now our two sets of eyes move to Holly's chest.

"But yours *are*!" I say. "They must be, because I'm using the secret weapons tonight."

"Think again, babe. I've got a pair and a spare." Holly smiles and then leans forward to reapply her lipstick. "What if I lost one in the pool? I always carry a pair and a spare."

"In the pool? More likely in the racing car driver's spa." I give Holly a look. Between practice sessions this afternoon, she'd ducked off to have a spa with the racing driver. A private spa. (He has the flashiest and most expensive suite on the ship.)

Holly looks over at me with one raised eyebrow. "I keep telling you. It was just a spa. Nothing else. Antonio is a perfect gentleman..." She pauses and looks thoughtful for a moment. "Well, most of the time."

Hmmm. I decide that maybe this is the right time to bring up the Nessa's Lessons in Love thing. With all her badminton and spa bookings, I haven't had a chance yet. Frankly, I'd been slightly freaked out by watching Holly make what could only be called a fool of herself at badminton. "Um, Holly?"

"Mmmhmmm?" she replies as she fluffs her hair.

"Nessa's Lessons in Love. If they're not working out for you..."

Holly waves a hand. "Oh, they're just a bit of fun. And *I'm* having fun. I'm lucky you reminded me that's what I should be doing."

"Well, that's good, but maybe if you toned it down a bit." My eyes widen as the phrase comes out of my mouth. Tone it down a bit? Who am I? My dad?

"Maybe." Holly keeps fluffing.

"I mean, a bit of flirting is good, but you don't want to look silly or anything."

"Of course not." Fluff, fluff, fluff.

"You seem to be spending a lot of time with Antonio. Maybe finding PM is going to be easier than we thought?" And maybe, if Holly finds herself a nice boyfriend, she won't need so much badminton coaching, or so many spas.

Holly sighs. "I hope that's true, but I have to remember that, this time around, I'm going to move a bit more slowly. No more rushing into engagements for me. I've learned my lesson. The hard way."

"But what if Antonio really is PM?"

Holly turns her whole body toward me. "But if he really is PM," she says, lisping, her mannerisms, her whole *being* changing before me, "he really will wait for me."

"Oh. My. God." My eyes practically pop out of their sockets, and I instantly forget all about my Nessa's Lessons in Love nagging. "How do you do that?" It's like Holly *is* Marilyn Monroe. We may both be dressed exactly like her—pink, blonde, and diamonds—but it's almost as if Holly's channeling the woman when she drops into character like that.

She laughs. "Years of practice. I used to make my family laugh themselves sick when I was little. I'd do impersonations of anyone and everyone they asked me to. Famous people, people we knew, whoever. They'd even get the neighbors over to watch sometimes, like I was a circus act. Anyway, enough about that. Are you ready?"

We both take a final look at ourselves in the mirror.

"I think so," I say. But really, I'm lying. I've never been less ready for anything in my life.

"I think I'm going to be sick," I say, clinging on to the black curtain in front of me for support. I take another peek out at the audience. There must be a few hundred people out there at least. "No, I really *am* going to be sick." I look around for a bucket (though what a bucket would be doing back here, I have no idea). Behind us, some guy with the most disgusting ventriloquist's dummy you've ever seen sniggers at me.

Holly throws him a look. "That's just wrong," she says, eyeing off the doll that he's got his hand stuck up.

"Hey!" he pipes up now. "It's a *dummy*."

She turns back to me, pats my back, and shakes her head. "What is it with those dummies? Why can't they ever make a nice-looking one? I mean, how could you sleep at night, knowing that thing was in your house?"

My thoughts exactly.

"Hey, he can hear you, you know." The guy looks first at Holly, then at the dummy, who looks back at him.

I shudder.

Holly just shakes her head. "Forget about them. Are you really going to be sick?" She keeps patting my back rhythmically.

I pause. Will the flow back down my throat. Take a deep breath. "I think I'm going to be okay."

"Good for you. Just don't think about it too hard. Just think about it as another rehearsal. It's when you think too hard that you lose it."

I roll my eyes. "Like you'd know! You're a natural!"

Holly snorts. "Is that what you think? I was petrified of performing for the longest time. Especially in plays. I used to throw up three or four times before I went on every night. Night after night. It can't have been good for me."

"Really?"

She gives me a look. "I'm not Wonder Woman, you know. I am a real person. I'm petrified now, in fact."

I forget about my own fear entirely when I hear this. "Really? Of performing in some silly talent quest?"

Holly shakes her head. "Did I say that? No. I'm scared that your dad's going to catch us. He'll never speak to me again if he sees you looking like this."

Now it's me who shakes my head. "Don't worry about it. He's working tonight."

"I certainly hope so. For my sake. No, actually, for both our sakes."

I forget how queasy I'm feeling and snort. "Can you see my dad looking for a good time and heading to the talent quest? I don't think so. He'd be more likely to be alphabetizing the magazines in the gift shop, for easy referencing."

Holly frowns now. "You're too hard on your dad, Nessa. You don't realize what a complete and utter sweetie he is." But then she can't help but giggle. "I can just imagine him doing that—alphabetizing the magazines."

"Believe me, I don't have to imagine. I've *seen* him doing it."

"Really?" Beside me, her eyes widen, Marilyn Monroe style.

"Well, no. But I could see he wanted to."

Holly giggles again.

"Stop it!" I say. "You're freaking me out. It's like Marilyn's really here."

"Sorry." Holly stops giggling.

"Marilyns?" A guy sticks his head back through the curtain and looks at us.

"Yes?" we say, in unison.

"You're on."

m

The great thing about being on stage is that the lights are so bright you can't actually see much beyond the first few rows of people. This, however, is scary enough for me—I haven't even performed in front of a number like the thirty people or so who fill up those rows, let alone a few hundred. Surprisingly, though, things go quite well. Like Holly told me to, I pretend we're rehearsing again. That it's just me and Holly in her suite, each wearing a ton of make-up, a very tight pink dress, a scratchy wig, and baking under a spotlight. Hmmm, sure. I think of Marilyn singing "Diamonds Are a Girl's Best Friend" in *Gentlemen Prefer Blondes,* and like Holly, I try to *be* her. Pink-outfitted, diamond-encrusted, man-hunting Lorelei.

Step, kick, step, kick...twirl and step and step...(quick, surreptitious check that bracelet and necklace are still attached)*...arms out, arms in, twirl again...*

By the time we're halfway through our little number, I'm even starting to enjoy myself a bit, and Holly gives me a big wink just as there's a flash from the audience. I look down to see the ship's photographer. Hey! It's Ted! Just like he'd promised, the photos of Holly and me had appeared under Dad and my cabin door the very same evening that I'd spoken to him. And not just one or two copies—ten copies! And a note, saying that if I wanted any more photos taken of Holly and me, just to let him know where and when we'd be doing things. Wasn't that nice of him? I flash him an extra big smile as Holly and I head into our finale.

Step, kick, step, kick...twirl and step and step...arms out, arms in, twirl again...

I really get into the spirit of the thing with our last sequence.

Twirl, kick, step, kick..."Diamonds!" I belt out. "Diamonds! Diamonds are a..." *twirl, kick, step, kick.* Wow. This is easier than I thought. This is fun. Maybe I *should* consider a career on the stage? *Twirl, kick, step, kick...*

Oh. Cancel that. Maybe I won't.

Because, oh.

Oh no.

No.

Dad alert. Dad alert.

And I must freeze slightly, because I think Holly notices, and her head turns to him only a fraction of a second after I do. He's hanging around the aisle in one of the front rows, searching for a seat. Someone hands him a program and he holds it up. At first quite close to his face and then a long way away. His glasses, I think to myself, trying to keep my steps in time with Holly's while, at the same time, Ted's camera flashes away, lighting us up even further. Making us even more obvious than two pink-outfitted, bewigged, diamond-encrusted girls can be. Hello! it says. Look at the girls on the stage! Pay attention to them! Eyes up here!

But me, my eyes stay on my father. What is he doing here? He starts along the row, goes to sit down, finds a spot, and then does the in/out/in of the program thing again. There's a word or two with the woman sitting next to him, who points out a line on the program and then he...oh, no...glances up.

Oh, no.

No.

He squints first at me, then at Holly, then looks back down again and does the in/out/in of the program one more time. And then, just when I think my time has run out, without a backward glance he gets up and starts to leave.

What? Hello? Dad! Over here! Daughter to be grounded! Maybe even for years!

I watch him come toward me, passing through the people in his row who obligingly lift their knees up (again) so he can pass. He's walking, walking, walking. Um, and the totally weird thing is—I don't think he's noticed I'm on stage at all.

"Diamonds!" I keep singing, trying not to rush through the song, even though my voice now sounds strangely wooden. *Step, kick, twirl*...There's another flash of Ted's camera and I decide just to go for it. To go for it and get off stage as fast as possible. I mean, what's going to happen is that my dad's going to look up right now. He's going to look up right now and see me, and reach up and drag me off the stage.

But he doesn't. He keeps moving along the row. Oh. Well, okay then. May as well go out with a bang.

And I do.

"Are a girl's best..." *Da, da-da, da, da, da-da, da, da-da, daaaaa*, the music fills the room and I fling my arms out, ready for the final pose.

Which is when it happens.

My dress pulls down as my arms go up and one of the chicken fillets goes flying through the air and lands...*thwack*...on my dad's balding head as he passes right in front of me on the stage.

"... best friend." I squeak my last line as Dad's eyes meet mine with another squint. Beside me, Holly is silent, her mouth in a small O.

There really is silence then. The music cuts out and, for a second, Holly and I just stand there on stage. Paralyzed in our final pose.

And I might have stayed there forever if Holly hadn't pulled herself together, reached over, grabbed me, hoisted me up, and dragged me off the stage. It isn't until we're peeking out from behind the curtain that the entire audience bursts out laughing.

Clinging on to the black curtain again, I groan. I groan long and loud. "I just want to die. I want to die right now. Please. It's not fair to keep me alive. It's not kind."

Holly looks over at me, still silent, her eyes wide, like before, but now not Marilyn-like. Instead they're more "I can't believe what just happened."

"Well..." she starts, but then pauses. "I guess I'm lucky I did bring a pair and a spare. I'll be needing that spare," she continues. And then she loses it.

But me, I'm not ready to laugh about anything.

The audience was ready years ago, however. Out in the ballroom, they keep laughing. And laughing. And laughing.

Really. I wouldn't complain if I dropped dead now. I really wouldn't.

"Oh, Nessa." Holly pats my arm. "Lighten up, sweetheart. You know something?"

"What?" I look over at her.

"Worse things have happened at sea." She screeches again.

I can't help but force back a chuckle when she says this. It's one of my dad's favorite sayings.

"At sea! At sea!" Holly's practically wetting herself she's laughing so hard now. I hope she brought other spares as well—like spare underwear.

I shake my head, but as I watch her, I just can't help myself. My little chuckle turns into a big chuckle, and then I start laughing. First normally, then harder and harder as I think about that chicken fillet flying through the air. And I may as well have a good laugh. When my dad finds me I probably won't just be grounded, I may never be allowed to laugh again.

Anyway, we laugh for ages. Until we almost *do* wet ourselves.

"You chicks are weird," the ventriloquist dummy guy says as he pushes past to go on stage. We stop laughing. Then...

"Chicks! Chicks! Chicken fillet!" Holly says, and we lose it all over again.

It takes us less than a minute of his act (that ugly dummy would sober anyone up) to pull ourselves together properly.

"Oh, boy..." Holly takes a deep breath, then another one, and leans against the wall, wiping a tear or two away from her face. "I don't think I've laughed that hard since...I don't know when." She leans forward, peeking out into the audience again. "Hey," she says, turning back towards me for a second. "Your dad's not there. He's gone."

I take a look myself. She's right. And then I groan again. "Probably because he's making his way back here to roast my drumsticks."

"Ha!" Holly laughs again, but then she stops. "No, wait. I was wrong. He *is* still there. He's waiting for the elevator." She turns back towards me again, a big grin on her face. "But it doesn't look like there's anything wrong. Nessa, I don't think he saw us!"

"No. I'm sure he did. He looked right at me." I move forward, jostling for space. It only takes me a second to spot him. He's waiting for the elevator now, the program doing the in/out/in thing again. "Oh!" I grab Holly's arms. "He really *didn't* see us! The thing is, he doesn't have his glasses, and he's as blind as a bat without them! All he would have seen is two big pink blobs!"

"But he was so close..." Holly peers out.

"I know! I thought he saw me when he passed in front, but the lights must've been too bright. Holly! He didn't see us!" I reach over and grab my pink partner in crime.

And then, with this realization, Holly and I spend the next thirty seconds dancing a little jig around the backstage area, dodging the next lot of contestants. "Oh, but stop!" Holly cries out as we go to take one more turn around. "We've got to get out of here. And quick. If your dad sees you in pink tonight and remembers what the song was, you're probably done for."

I nod. She's right. We take off fast. And we don't stop running until we get to Holly's suite.

Eight

It takes us all of two minutes to wrench our clothes off, pull the wigs and bobby pins off our heads, take Holly's jewelry off (still on my neck and wrist, thank goodness), wrestle some jeans and shirts on, and slap baseball caps over our flattened hair. We look like we've spent the evening watching movies in Holly's suite. Just like I'd told my dad I would be doing.

We're tissuing the last of the make-up off when there's a knock on the door. Still hyped up and jittery, the first thing we both do is panic. "Who could it be?!" I grab Holly's arm and our eyes meet in the bathroom mirror.

"I don't know! I don't know!" She grabs mine back.

"Should we answer it?"

Holly opens her mouth to answer, when a voice calls out. "Delivery, Ms. Isles."

Our bodies relax. A delivery? Well, phew.

Shaking her head, Holly goes over to open the door while I wait in the lounge room. "Yes? Oh! No, I'll take them..."

She comes back inside carrying two bunches of flowers. One absolutely gigantic bunch and a smaller one, which is still huge. They're both stuffed full of pink flowers. All kinds of pink—shocking pink, pastel pink, candy pink, and so on. On the way back over, she reads the attached card out loud: "For the most exquisite pink petals...Love always, Antonio." She brings the larger bunch up to her face to smell them. "Oh, aren't they gorgeous, Nessa?"

I nod. "They're beautiful. I can't believe he sent me flowers as well. And I can't believe how quickly they arrived."

Holly's eyes widen. "Those Italians, they don't mess around, do they?"

This time, I shake my head. "If this is anything to go by, we should have you engaged in the next half-hour, married tomorrow morning, and your first child graduating from college by the end of the cruise."

Holly laughs and comes over to give me the smaller bunch of flowers. "For a moment there I was sure it was going to be your dad."

"You and me both."

Her eyes move toward the phone on the bench beside us. "You know what? You should call the cabin and see if he's there. At least it'll put your mind at rest."

"You think?"

Holly nods and passes me the phone. "Here," she says. "I'll take the flowers and put them in some water."

"I'd better leave them here, I think," I tell her. "I can't take them to our cabin. Too many questions. Anyway, I don't think they'd fit."

"Good idea." Holly moves off as I dial. "I hadn't thought about that."

My dad picks up after half a ring (like I said, that cabin is *small*).

"Hey, Dad, it's me!" I say before he can even get a word in. "How's it going? Working away? I thought you might be bored. Did you want to come up and watch another movie with us?" (I try not to brag about it, but I'm an excellent liar. It comes with being an only child.)

"Oh, Nessa. You know, the strangest thing just happened..."

I hold my breath, my eyes fixed on a certain point on the wall in front of me. Here it comes. He knows. He knows, and I'm grounded forever.

"I went up to the talent quest they're having tonight—one of my subjects is participating in it and I thought I might be able to include it in my research as she's never really done anything like this before. Anyway, I got all the way up there when I realized I'd forgotten my glasses."

"Oh, um, really? Isn't that strange. Ha ha."

"Hmmm? Not really. That's not the strange thing, you see. I took a seat, just for a minute. There was some very silly act on. Two floozies dancing around the stage. But I stayed in case my subject's act was the next one on as this one was ending."

Floozies? Hey! That's not very nice. But I hold my breath again. Sometimes my dad likes to play this game—he holds off and holds off, seeing if I'll confess to whatever I've done before he gets to the kicker. It's torture. I'm sure they used something like it in the Spanish Inquisition. Torture by father.

"And then you know what happened?"

I shake my head, then realize my dad can't see me. "No," I squeak, just like I'd squeaked my last line on stage. "Um, no," I cough, repeating the word in my normal voice.

"This...this thing flew out and hit me on the head. I'm holding it now. But Nessa, for the life of me, I can't make out what it is. It's pink and made of plastic—a soft plastic—and on one side there's a little raised lump. Very strange. A very strange object indeed."

I suck my breath in hard. Oh boy. He doesn't know. He really doesn't know. And this is too much. Too much! I try very, very hard not to laugh now. Because my dad might not know what that raised lump is, but I do—he's talking about the little fake nipple! Oh, no. I'm going to laugh again any second now. And just when I think I'm going to lose it, the phone is wrenched from my hand.

"William, how *are* you?!...Yes, we're having a lovely time thanks...No, she's not being any trouble at all...Really? That's strange...Soft plastic, did you say? With a raised lump?...Well, my advice would be to throw it out. After all, you never know where it's been. Anyway, must go. Nessa's starting the next movie up. I'll see you later!"

I sink down to the floor, as does Holly when she's put the phone down. It's like our knees can't hold us up anymore.

"Soft plastic!" Holly looks at me.

"Raised lump!" I look back.

"Nipple!" we say together. And I think we're about to lose it one more time (seriously, I think I've broken several ribs from all the laughing I've been doing this evening), when there's another knock on the door. This time from the door that joins Holly's room to Marc's.

That shuts us up. Fast.

"Holly! Holly Thelma Isles! Are you in there?" It's Marc.

"Thelma?" I look over at her. "*Thelma*?!" It's nice to know someone else gets the middle name treatment besides me. But *Thelma*? And from her *nephew*?!

We do the paralyzed thing again. Honestly, we're like a pair of deer in the headlights (or should that be spotlights!) tonight.

"I know you're in there! I'm coming in!"

Still paralyzed, sitting on the floor, the two of us watch the doorknob turn. As the door itself starts to open, Holly accidentally snorts. Which, of course, sets me off again.

When I finally finish with my latest set of giggles, Marc is standing over both of us.

"What are you doing?" he asks, looking first at Holly, then at me. From the tone in his voice, you'd think we were doing something criminal. Not sitting on the floor in Holly's suite yukking it up.

"We're...we're just..." Holly starts.

"We're just having a good time." I give him an exasperated look.

He gives me one right back. "Oh, come on, Nessa. How dumb do you think I am? It's all over the ship. I didn't mean what are you doing here, in Holly's suite, on the floor, laughing like a pair of hyenas. I know exactly what you're doing here. You're hiding out. What I meant was, what do you think you're doing making complete asses of yourselves at the talent quest? I mean, honestly, Holly. You're supposed to be lying low. Not shaking your booty all over the boat."

Holly and I collapse into a fit of giggles again. Shaking your booty? And what's the plural of booty, anyway? Booties?

"Oh, stop it," he says, crossly.

Holly and I both bite our lips and do as we're told.

"I can't believe you!" Marc throws one hand up.

Holly sighs then. "Marc, it was completely innocent. Well, except for the bit where Nessa lost her breast!"

Marc's eyes move to my chest for a second and then zip away again. Hey! Do you mind? "Thanks a lot," I say, and hit Holly on the arm.

"Sorry."

It's Marc who snorts now. "Yes. You'll definitely be sorry tomorrow. When the photos are all over the papers."

There's a pause and then Holly shrugs. "They're always all over the papers whatever I do. At least I'll be looking like I'm having a good time after this break-up. Last time it was all horrible photos of me looking cold and miserable in coffee shops in Vienna without make-up on."

I watch her expression as she says this—the flip of her hand, the toss of her hair—and realize this is what she was talking about before. The "devil may care" thing. Ah, so that's what she meant.

"Holly, you just can't..." Marc shakes his head, and I turn to see him looking really quite angry now, when there's a knock on the door to the suite. All three of our heads whip around to face the sound.

Holly goes to get up, but Marc shakes his head again. "I'll get it."

He goes over, opens the door and I hear him talking to someone who replies curtly. There's no mistaking the voice, though.

It's Antonio.

When the door opens fully and he sees us, he ignores Marc, pushing past him to get into the room. He strides over to us (Antonio seems to do everything at great speed, even walking and talking and flower sending) and when he reaches us, claps his hands in delight. "*Bellissima*! *Bellissima*! The performance of the century! Now, we will go out and celebrate. Yes? The night, she is young and full of promise!"

"Uh uh, not so fast. I don't think anybody's going anywhere." Marc steps between him and the two of us on the floor.

Antonio takes a step back, and he and Marc look at each other for a moment or two as if they're about to butt horns. Before they can, however, Holly stands up and then gives me a hand up as well. "You know what?" she says to no-one in particular. "I've had a really good time tonight. I'm sick of worrying about what people are going to say, or think, or write about me. If I worried about that, I'd go to bed right now, like a good girl. But I don't feel like going to bed. So I'm going out, with Antonio." Her eyes flash rebelliously at Marc when she says this. "And I'm going to have a good time."

Antonio takes a step toward Holly and claps his hands again joyously. "But of course we will have a good time! Everyone has a good time with Antonio!"

So I've heard, I think. (Cruise gossip travels fast.)

Holly turns to me now. "How about you, Nessa?"

I pause. Like they say, two's company, three's a crowd. "Oh, no. I can't. I have to go back and check in with my dad and get my good girl hours up. Thanks for the flowers, though, Antonio. They're beautiful."

"Oh!" Holly jumps and we all turn and look at her. For a second, I wonder if something's bitten her. "Oh, um, yes, I just meant..." And then, right before my eyes, all of our eyes, she changes again. Morphs into this completely different person. "*Darling*, they're beautiful!" she simpers. "They smell divine. You're a pet. A complete pet." She reaches over and rests a hand on Antonio's chest for just a second too long. "I'll just freshen myself up."

I look over at Antonio and see that he's happily lapping up every word and is ready to go back for at least six more courses. But Marc...uh oh. His face is scrunched up to the point where he looks like he needs his appendix removed in under thirty seconds, or else.

As for me, I don't quite know what to think. It's like when I was watching Holly this afternoon at badminton. Holly was putting Nessa's Lessons in Love into action and they seemed to be working on the guys. A little too well, in my opinion. So why, if everything is working out as planned, and everyone's getting what they want (well, except for Marc), does it feel so wrong? Maybe I should have tried harder to talk to her about it earlier tonight?

"I won't be a minute." Antonio gets a hug now (and, um, it's not from Marc).

Hmmm...time to go, I think.

"Yes, thanks for the flowers, Antonio," I say again, quickly this time, and Antonio looks down, remembering there are other people in the room besides him and Holly.

"It is my pleasure, littlest petal." He bends over, and before I know what's happening, has kissed me first on one cheek, then the other, then on the first cheek again.

"Oh, thanks..." I'm not quite sure where to look. Note to Nessa: In future dating life, beware of Italians. They make your head spin. "I'd, um, best be going." I start toward the door. "Thanks for the great evening, Holly. Bye Antonio. Bye Marc." I wave at Holly and Antonio and then walk even faster toward the door when I see Marc's expression. Now he's moved on from appendix-removal land and looks like Vesuvius on a hot summer's day.

When I close the suite door behind me, I breathe a sigh of relief. Phew. What an evening. In fact, it's turned into such an evening I have to stand there, leaning against the door for a minute or two, trying to get my head together as I think back over Holly and my number at the talent quest, my dad turning up, the flying chicken fillet, Dad not spotting us (hello?! I still can't believe my luck!), the flowers, and now Marc having a tantrum. Definitely an evening to remember! And I guess we'll see how successful our song and dance routine was tomorrow—when just about every guy on the boat will have an icebreaker to approach Holly with. I can almost see it now: "I loved your act, Holly!"; "That number was a scream, Holly"; "I had such a laugh, Holly!"

Right. Feeling a bit more on top of things now, I push myself off the door and start down the corridor. But I only get as far as the elevators when I hear footsteps running toward me. I turn to see Marc. "Oh, um, hi."

"Don't 'Um, hi' me." He still looks furious.

"What?"

"Was this all your idea?"

I look at him, but don't say anything. After the show we've just witnessed in there, it's probably not the best time to tell Marc about Nessa's Lessons in Love. One, it's a girl thing, however misguided it's starting to feel. Two, I don't think he'd be very understanding.

"I thought as much."

I watch him for a moment longer (waiting for either lava or steam to come out of his ears), and then I shrug and try to play it cool. "I just thought the talent quest would be fun. We both had a good time. I don't see what the problem is."

"The *problem*, littlest petal," Marc spits, "is that Holly's not supposed to be making an exhibition of herself. The *problem* is that she is, like I said, supposed to be lying low."

I shrug again, which I can see just makes Marc even more furious. "I take it Holly knows that. Isn't it her decision to go in the talent quest or not then?" I feel a little bit bad saying this, because I know Holly didn't enter the competition for all the right reasons, but Marc's over-reacting a tad, too.

"Of course it's her decision, but it's probably not a good idea to *encourage* her. And why is she acting so strangely, huh? What's up with that?"

I pause and think about how I'm going to handle this. "Strangely?"

Marc shakes his head at me. "Oh, come on, Nessa. You can't say you didn't see that in there. With Antonio. And I overheard some people today talking about how they'd seen her playing badminton. It sounded like she was wearing practically nothing and acting like an idiot. It's as if she's turning into this whole other person. I asked her about it, but she denied everything."

Um, er. "Maybe she's just having a good time..."

Now it's Marc who pauses. "Wait a second. You were there, weren't you, this afternoon?"

Um, um. "For a while."

"Has this all got something to do with you as well, her acting strangely?"

Oh, my.

"Nessa, what's going on?"

I take a deep breath and face Marc squarely. "Marc, you're being silly. There's nothing "going on" as you put it. Holly's just having a good time. That's what cruises are for, right? To have a good time. Let your hair down. Act ridiculously on stage. Just lighten up, okay?"

Silence.

And then Marc starts shaking his head, slowly at first, but then faster. His eyes have narrowed until they're now just small slits. "Oh, listen to you. You really think you're *it*, don't you? That you're Holly's best buddy and—"

I butt in, fast, wanting to stop his train of thought right here. "No, it's not that. I'm not expecting anything from Holly. We'll probably never see each other again after next week. The talent quest entry was just an idea that popped into my head. I thought we'd have fun. That's all, Marc. Really, that's all." Well, this is half true—have fun *and* meet all the men on the boat, that is. I have to look away, I'm telling so many lies.

"Yeah, right. As far as I can see you've had a few too many good ideas lately. I just don't get it, Nessa. I thought we were friends. I thought that you...that we..." He trails off.

A few too many good ideas? What's that supposed to mean? Our eyes meet again as Marc stops speaking, and suddenly, his expression changes. Instead of anger, there's now disappointment and confusion. He turns then and heads off back down the corridor.

"Marc?" I call after him, realizing what he's just said. I take a few steps forward. "Marc, of course we're friends. Don't be silly. And what do you mean? You thought that I, that we...what?"

But his slump-shouldered, retreating figure doesn't turn around. And all I get is a shake of one hand in reply.

Nine

I trudge back to the cabin, pick Holly's chicken fillet out of the wastepaper basket, and stick it under my pillow where Dad won't find it. And maybe it's the chicken fillet making my pillow lumpy, I don't know, but I *do* know I don't sleep well that night. I can't stop thinking about Marc. Not about him lecturing Holly, or lecturing me for signing us up for the talent quest, but about that figure that retreated down the hallway. He looked so...defeated. And that look of disappointment on his face before he left. As if I'd turned out to be someone he thought I wasn't.

Anyway, I don't think it's the chicken fillet stopping me from getting any rest. I think it's me realizing that Marc feels hurt. And left out. And as if he doesn't know everything that's going on. Which he doesn't, of course. And it's all because of me.

As soon as I'm up and showered, I give his room a call, hoping we can have a chat and sort things out. But his answering service is switched on. I leave a message, asking him to give me a call. After breakfast, I leave another message. After lunch, I leave another.

Okay. Something tells me Marc's avoiding me.

Mid-afternoon, Holly calls me, and we arrange to have a quick cocktail/mocktail at our usual spot.

"Congratulations!" is the first thing Holly says to me, jumping into my line of view.

I squint up at her from my sun lounge, bringing my hand up to shade my eyes from the sun. "Congratulations for what?"

She passes something to me. A piece of paper.

"We won the talent quest! It's a one-hundred-dollar drink voucher. All yours."

"We won?!" I sit straight up, looking first at the voucher, then up at Holly.

"Of course! You didn't think that guy with the ugly dummy was going to win, did you? Or the kid with the spoons? Or the girl with the flying prosthesis?"

"Oh, very funny. Ha, ha, ha." I give her a look as she dumps her raffia bag on the deck and sits down beside me. "We have to split it, though. It's half yours."

She shakes one hand. "Don't be silly. It was your idea. And they give me everything for free, anyway. It's ridiculous what I get for free these days. Dresses, drinks, meals. And I can afford it now! I wish I could go back in time and give half the stuff I get for free now to starving-actress me ten years ago."

I nod.

"I'll tell you something, though. That act worked like a treat. I can't believe how many dates I've been asked out on today. I'm pretty much booked solid for the rest of the trip!"

"No way!"

"Oh, definitely way. Breakfasts and lunches and trips off the boat. All kinds of things."

"Well, that's good."

Holly pauses.

"Isn't it?"

She pauses again, looking at me, and then nods slowly. "It's getting...a bit tiring."

Oh, no. Have I done the wrong thing? I remember how I felt yesterday, watching Holly throw the badminton game. And seeing her act so strangely with Antonio. "But if you don't want to do anything, if you don't want to go on any of the dates, don't go. I didn't mean to...I..."

Holly reaches over and pats my arm. "No. It's fine. I'm having a good time. Like the lessons state, keep it light. That's what I want just now. Light and easy with no commitments. It's been good for me to talk to so many new people. It's just that sometimes I find myself sizing them all up because it makes me remember that, in my heart, I'm still looking for...um..."

"The One?" I try. "Perfect Man?"

Holly nods, her face glum. "That's him. PM."

I pat her arm. "Don't worry. You'll find him. I know you will. He's somewhere here on this ship. I just know it."

Beside me, Holly shrugs a small shrug. "I can only hope that's true."

It's awful to see her looking so miserable. "You know what I think?"

"What?" She turns to face me again.

"I think you really should try toning it down a bit. I mean, when I was watching you yesterday, it kind of freaked me out. Throwing that badminton game—you can't really have liked doing that."

Holly shakes her head and laughs lightly. "No, I can't say I did."

"No. It wasn't very you. And why should you have to, anyway?"

Holly gives me a weird look now. "So, what are you saying? That we should just forget the whole Nessa's Lessons in Love deal?"

Yes. "Um...I'm not sure. Maybe if you just tone it down a bit."

Holly sighs. "Tone it down a bit. That was my parents' favorite saying when I was growing up. 'Holly Thelma Isles, tone it down a bit!'"

I look over at her incredulously. "Really?"

She nods. "Why?"

"That's my dad's favorite saying. Well, except his is: 'Nessa Joanne Mulholland, tone it down a bit!'"

"Joanne, huh? I'll swap you."

I shake my head and laugh. "Thelma? I don't think so. Anyway, like you were saying, why don't you just try keeping things light and fun, but forget all the subservient stuff. That's the stuff I hate seeing."

Holly snorts. "That's the stuff I hate *doing*. I could have creamed them all at badminton. I think I've just got to take a step back for a while. Be me. And not worry about..." She pauses.

"Boys?"

She shrugs.

"Men?"

"I guess that's the word I'm looking for."

I nod decisively. "Right then. Step one, stop looking for PM, and step two, just try having a good time."

"It sounds so simple when you say it like that."

"Like you told me, try not to think about it so hard. Go with the flow, as they say. Think you can give it a whirl?"

Holly nods once more.

Well, good. Time to change the topic, I think. "Hey, I just remembered. I've got something for you, as well."

This cheers her up a bit. "What's that?"

I reach into my pocket and pull it out.

"Oh! Edwina!"

This makes me pause. "Edwina?"

Holly nods. "Edwina and Lucy are my spares. This is Edwina. Edwina, meet Nessa."

"I think we've already met," I laugh. "Intimately."

Suddenly, a shadow looms over the two of us. Well, the three of us (Holly, me and Edwina). "Ladies. Can I offer you something to drink?" It's the scary drinks waiter.

"Hmmm," Holly says, still holding Edwina out (nipple up) and not making any moves to put her away. "I think I'll have a peach and mango smoothie, my good man."

"I'll have a tab, thanks," I say. "And I don't mean the kind that comes in a can. It's Nessa Mulholland. Cabin 252b." I pass him the voucher. "To start, I'd like to put a strawberry frappé on it, please."

"Of course, ladies." The scary drinks waiter turns and heads off.

"Oh, and a bowl of maraschino cherries, as well!" I say as he goes.

Beside me, Holly nods. "Good call," she says. And we both settle back for an hour or two of afternoon drinks and gossip.

We're halfway through our second round of drinks when I spot them. The young couple, off to our right, taking photos of us. "You've seen them, have you?" Holly says to me, without turning around to look. "They've been there for at least ten minutes, snapping away. I hope they got a good close-up of my leg-hair stubble."

"Ten minutes? Really?" I hadn't noticed them until now. Then again, I hadn't noticed Holly's leg-hair stubble, either.

"You develop a special kind of vision in this game. A wider kind of vision. In case one of them has a knife, or something worse."

"A knife?!" This makes me sit up a bit. I twist around to have a better look at them.

"No, it's okay. The one with the knife's still in jail. I hope. Oh, look. They're going. Good."

She's right; they are walking off now they've been spotted. But when I turn around again, I can't do anything but sit, mutely, and look at Holly. Her words have sunken in, and now I don't know what to say. Those people. I've just realized something—how are they any different from me? I mean, why am I sitting here with Holly and they're over there? And maybe Holly sees this written all over my face, because she moves into action, swinging her legs around off her sun lounge and placing them onto the deck beside me so we're sitting much closer together.

"I knew we should have talked about this sooner. I guess this is all a bit weird for you, Nessa."

Still mute, I nod as I look into her eyes. The eyes I've seen on a million movie posters.

"I mean, you must wonder what I'm doing. An old pathetic person hanging around with you, cramping your style."

What? My eyes go round now. Hang on a minute. Holly thinks she's cramping my style? As if! And she's not old. Or pathetic. Holly's...amazing. Just amazing. I go to open my mouth, but she shakes her head, and I realize she wants to say something important, so I let her continue.

"You've just got this really great take on life, Nessa. Your whole Marilyn thing—it's just awesome. Not to mention trying to find PM for me. And it's so refreshing that you don't...hmmm... how can I put this? That you don't want anything from me. Adults always *want* something from me. Not that you're a kid, of course I'm not saying that. What I mean is you're not old and jaded and only out for yourself." Holly looks at her hands for a moment. "I just feel like I can tell you things and you won't, you know, betray me. Oh, I don't mean *betray*, it's too strong a word..." She shrugs and looks up again to give me a small smile. "Am I making any sense at all here?"

I think for a moment, trying to force my brain into accepting what my ears are hearing, but eventually I manage to answer. "Yeah. Yeah, you are."

Holly sighs and reaches out to grab both my hands. "Don't get old and jaded, Nessa. Hold on to you if you can. Hold on to you and how you look at things. It's important to remember who you are inside. Sometimes, as you get older, you forget. And that would be a great shame in your case." She repositions herself and then takes a deep breath. "Ugh. I'm sounding a bit like Yoda, aren't I? Sorry."

I shake my head, our eyes finally breaking contact. "No," I say. "What you just said—I think that's the nicest thing anyone's ever said to me."

Holly smiles. "Well, good. Because I meant it. Every word and...oh."

"What?" I say, but then follow Holly's eyes across the deck. It's Ted.

"Oh, no. It's Ted," she says with a groan.

I turn to face her again. "Don't you like him?" How could anybody not like Ted? He's such a sweetie. I still can't get over the fact he gave me ten copies of that photo.

"Who? Ted? It's not that I don't like him, he's just...like my shadow. After five years it gets a bit boring."

Five years? Huh? "What do you mean?"

Holly sits up a bit. "Ted. You know, my personal paparazzo."

Oh. Oh, no. "What?" I only just manage to get the word out, my mouth is hanging so far open.

"Hi, Ted!" Holly calls out now, and Ted runs off.

I'm not sure what to say. All the things I've told him—my name, who my dad is, what Holly and I have been doing—they all whiz through my head at a million miles an hour. "I thought he was the ship's photographer," I end up saying quietly. And how idiotic am I? No wonder he was so surprised that first time I met him. My asking how much his photos cost. Wince. And where I could find them. Double wince. No wonder he acted so weird—he probably thought I was going to chuck his camera overboard and run off to search his cabin for film. How embarrassing.

"What's the matter?" Holly looks over at me.

"Oh, nothing. Nothing. I was just thinking it must be awful, having someone follow you around all the time. As in, professionally. Not just like the people before."

Holly shrugs. "Well, yes. But I'm lucky. Ted's a really nice guy. A sweetie. Very shy, though."

I wince again now. A sweetie. Just like I'd thought. But, hang on. "Shy?" I say. After all, shy doesn't exactly fit in with the job description.

"Well, with me, anyway. Just look at him!"

I look over to the far side of the deck and spot Ted—peering around a corner, camera at the ready.

"Really, I'm very lucky. And you can't tell me he's not cute."

She's right. I forgot to mention that the other day. Ted actually is super-cute, with gorgeous wavy brown hair and brown-flecked green eyes.

"I think it's the tan that really sets him apart. All that waiting around for me outside movie studios and the like," Holly continues.

She's right again. He does have a nice tan. Which sets off his green eyes perfectly.

"Hmmm. If he wasn't my personal paparazzo, I'd have invited him out for dinner a long time ago, I think."

I turn and look at Holly now. "Why don't you? It'd save him chasing after you for one evening at least."

Holly laughs. "No, I couldn't. It'd be too...weird. And, I mean, if it worked out, he'd have to quit, wouldn't he? And then I might get an awful personal paparazzo like that ugly, rude one that my friend—"

For the second time this afternoon, a shadow falls over us and we both look up.

Unfortunately, this time, it's not the drinks waiter.

It's Marc.

Oh.

He moves over beside Holly's sun lounge and ignores me when I say hello.

"Hey!" Holly says. "Guess who was just here? Ted!"

Marc groans. "Great. That's all I need."

I wince when I hear this and wonder if I should come clean about Ted. To both of them. But no. I'd just look stupid, wouldn't I? How was I to know that Ted was a paid-up member of the paparazzi? I thought he was the ship's photographer and that getting Holly seen would lead to more male meetings, if you know what I mean.

"Well," Holly says, putting her drink down on the table in between us. "I'd better run. I've got three dates tonight."

"Three?!" Marc and I say at the same time. I look up at him when this happens, but he keeps right on ignoring me.

Holly laughs. "It sounds a bit much, doesn't it? I've got drinks, then dinner, then more drinks lined up. Oh, Nessa, tell your dad I'm sorry I couldn't make it again, won't you?"

Huh? My dad? He hadn't told me he'd invited Holly to dinner again. "Um, sure," I say.

Marc shoots me another filthy look. What? He's got a problem with my dad now? I roll my eyes. Who knows what's going on in his head?

"I'd better make all those drinks sparkling mineral water, though. I've got a film set to be on in six weeks. Can't completely let myself go." She jumps up so she's next to Marc. "Okay, see you, Nessa! I won't forget: no PM, have a good time. No PM, have a good time."

"Um, great. That's great. Bye Holly," I say. Holly waves at me. "Bye Marc." No reaction here. "Bye Edwina."

This, at least, makes him turn around. Holly laughs, and Marc gives me a quick glance.

"No PM? What's PM? Have a good time? And who's Edwina?" I hear him say as he and Holly make their way across the deck toward the stairs.

Ten

Again, it comes to me in the middle of the night. With the ship's engine going full steam ahead next to my left eardrum, I sit up straight in bed, just like last time. (Why it always happens in the middle of the night, I'll probably never know.)

This time, the Marilynism practically winds me.

How could I not have seen it sooner? How could I not have picked up the clues? The signs were all there, clear as day. Bigger signs even than the Hollywood one that Holly lives under.

No wonder Nessa's Lessons in Love felt so wrong and didn't work out. Aside from being ridiculous, it wasn't the answer.

The answer was always there. I just didn't realize it.

But now I've found it: it's Ted. Ted is the answer.

Like I said, how could I not have seen it sooner? After all, it's too *Gentlemen Prefer Blondes* to be true. I'm Lorelei and Holly is Dorothy, and Ted...Ted is the private detective. The guy who ran around taking the photos of the girls on the cruise ship. Ugh, what's his name again? Starts with an M or something. Hang on...Malone. That's it! Ernie Malone.

Oh, this is too much. Too much! First, Holly knowing the line from the movie when we were boarding the boat, the two of us being on a cruise ship together, her meeting up with me on the sun lounges, her need to find a decent guy, and now Ted.

I've been going down the wrong track trying to get Holly to meet every man on board. The right man's been under my nose (and her house's front hedge) all the time. And isn't that typical? Isn't that how it happens in all the great romances? In novels and movies and, oh, everything? It's always the guy who's been there all along that the heroine ends up with. Always!

Holly's words from this afternoon come back to me now...*A really nice guy, a sweetie, you can't tell me he's not cute, I'd have invited him out for dinner*...Oh, it really is too good to be true. Holly likes him! Holly likes Ted!

Oh. Wait. Hang on.

I remember something else then. Not Holly's words, but Marc's. From the other night at dinner. *What she needs is a guy who isn't in the industry at all. A guy who isn't even interested in it. But she never meets anyone who isn't in the industry. If she's got any hope of having a lasting relationship, she needs to meet different kinds of men. All sorts of men.*

Ted. Ted's in the industry, I realize.

Oh.

I lie back down, stare at the ceiling, and think about this for a minute. The other night, I'd totally agreed with Marc. And even now, something's telling me—my gut, I think—that maybe I still think he's right. It'd be good for Holly to have someone who wouldn't want to use her and her contacts. Yes, it would be good...but maybe it just won't happen that way. After all, Ted has to be right for Holly, he has to be! There are too many Marilynisms for it to be wrong. It's just like *Gentlemen Prefer Blondes*. It's meant to be.

I quiet Marc's words that are still reverberating in my head. I stop listening to my gut. Yes. It's meant to be. I have to make it happen. That's why I'm here. When Holly said all that stuff about me this afternoon, about being myself, she meant it. And there's no doubting it in my mind—we met for a reason and this is it.

Right. It's going to take a lot of work, but I'm going to have to make it happen, or it might not happen at all.

Holly's future happiness depends upon it.

When I wake up, my dad's gone. There's a note on his bed saying he's got a few people to interview and he'll be back later (and that I should behave myself). I phone Holly to find out how her dates went last night, but she doesn't answer. So, with nothing else to do, I take a quick shower and head upstairs, pick up a croissant and a banana, skim the papers, and then head on over to aqua aerobics.

Holly and I have done it twice already, and both times we were the youngest in the pool by about thirty years (that's including Holly), not to mention the only people not wearing those funny flowery bathing caps. You know the ones? They look like rubber bath mats that sit on your head. Anyway, we liked it because we could pretend we were exercising and doing something good for ourselves and still chat at the same time.

Halfway through the class, I'm doing a "mule kick" (don't ask), and as I bend upright again, I glance up at the deck above us. I then stop mule kicking, or any kind of kicking, immediately. Because there, walking past on the deck above is Holly and my dad. Talking and laughing again. Just like the other day. I wonder what they're talking about. Oh, no, I hope it's not the study. I'd forgotten all about that, to tell the truth. Come to think of it, what am I doing mule kicking around a pool? I've got things to do—I've got to get Holly off Dad's study, and I've got to come up with some kind of a plan that will see Holly and Ted completely and utterly and foolishly in love by the end of this trip. Hey! Maybe I'll be able to swing it so the second problem cancels out the first one.

I glance up again and watch the two of them for a bit longer. Well, at least she's faring better by toning down the Nessa's Lessons in Love thing. Because, up there, Holly's not being anybody but herself. Like she is with me. There's no flirting, no Miss Clumsy, no "Ooohhh I can't play badminton because I'm just a silly girl." Not that she'd do that with my dad. After all, he's hardly PM material, isn't he? But it's nice to see Holly look herself again. At ease and happy and *really* having a good time.

"Umph," I say, as one of the little old ladies hits my back.

"Come on, Nessa!" the instructor yells out. "Olive's putting you to shame and she's eighty-three next week. You can kick harder than that, girlfriend. Let's step it up!"

Over the next day or so, I try to forget Marc's words (it's not hard, as he's still completely ignoring me), and I spend a lot of time tipping Ted the personal paparazzo off as to where Holly will be and when, in the hope that their eyes will meet across a crowded deck and they'll fall instantly in love. (I wish it was that easy.)

He turns up at breakfast (surprisingly, even when Holly slums it with me, rather than going to the swanky restaurant); he turns up at aqua aerobics (nice board shorts, Ted!); and he even turns up a few minutes before Holly's appointment with the pilates instructor, which looks kind of weird (oops).

It's the second day of Operation Tipping Off Ted, and Holly and I are heading up for our usual round of afternoon cocktails/mocktails when we notice someone sitting in our spot. My spot, actually.

"Hey!" Holly says, turning to me and looking almost as affronted as I feel. But then we see who it is.

Marc. Uh oh, my gut says to my brain.

"Well, well, well, if it isn't the three stooges," he says.

"Three?" Holly says, taking a look behind us.

"You're a bit late. But Ted was early. It's funny how Ted's always early these days, isn't it? Anyway, he had to leave." Marc gives me a look. A very *definite* look.

Oops.

He jumps up off his (*my*) chair now and takes my arm, leading me away. "I've just got to have a little chat with Nessa," he says to Holly.

"Um, sure. If you say so. Want me to order you guys something?"

"No, we're fine," Marc says, still leading me away. "Aren't we, Nessa?"

It doesn't look like it, I think to myself. As for my gut, it's too busy doing cartwheels to reply.

We keep walking till we get to the railing on the opposite side of the boat. *I hope he's not going to throw us overboard*, my brain says to my gut. *I wish I hadn't eaten that second fajita at lunch*, my gut replies.

Marc stops and faces me, looking me straight in the eye. "Are you tipping off Ted?"

Um, wow. Get straight to the point, why don't you? And, now, I don't know where to look. I try the deck. Then the ocean. "What? What are you talking about?" I finally manage to say.

Marc slaps the railing. "I knew it! I knew it! How could you do that, Nessa?"

"Knew what? Do what?" I look at him now.

"Oh, come on. You know what I'm talking about. Ted's been turning up all over the place for the last couple of days. It's weird. But then I realized what was even weirder was it's only been happening at places *you* know Holly's going to be at."

I look out at the ocean again. "Why would I do that? Why would I tell Ted where Holly's going to be all the time?"

There's a pause. A long pause.

"Oh, I don't know, Nessa. Maybe for *money*?"

What? It takes me a few moments to register what Marc's just said. But when I do, I snap to attention. And then I do look at Marc. Right at him. My eyes bore into his. "I am *not* taking any money from Ted. I'm not that kind of person." I take a step forward, closer towards him. Then another one. I try to catch my breath. "Got it? I wouldn't do that to Holly. *Ever*." My cheeks and my ears feel hot. Too hot, as if they're about to burn off. And as the words exit my mouth, I feel strangely detached. I don't ever remember being this angry before. Not in all my life. No-one's ever accused me of betraying a friend like Marc's accusing me of. For money. It's just wrong. I could never do it. And my dad...he's always brought me up to believe that money isn't everything. It isn't. I know it isn't. And that's why I'd never do what

Marc's just accused me of doing. I can't believe he's just said this to me. I take another step forward, about to lay into him again when he speaks.

"I..." Marc starts, then stops, as I think we both suddenly realize how close together we're standing. Our noses are practically touching and I can smell him—salty and warm as if he's just been for a dip in the pool.

My heart stops beating, pauses for a second, then begins racing crazily.

Oh my god, my brain says. *His head. It's tilting. He's going to...he's going to kiss you.*

Ugh, I really wish I hadn't had that second fajita, my stomach replies.

And then, in that moment that feels like several, it's my stomach I listen to. Quickly, awkwardly, I take two steps back. "I...I can't believe you said that about me." I look out across the ocean again, crossing my arms. And I can't. I can't believe anyone would think that about me, let alone Marc. What's gone wrong between us? Just a few days ago, we were getting along so well. Even if I didn't remain friends with Holly after the trip I thought that Marc and I definitely would, and now...oh, no. I think I'm going to cry.

Marc must see this. "I'm sorry, Nessa. I didn't think you'd do something like that, but there's something going on. I know that much. Can you tell me what it is?"

There's another long pause. And then, still not looking at him, I shake my head.

When I finally look back over again, Marc's gone.

That night, trying to sort everything out in my head, I write a super-long email to Alexa telling her everything that's gone on. I tell her about the Marilynisms. I tell her about Nessa's Lessons in Love. I tell her about Holly and Antonio and Ted, and Dad's study, and Marc, and how a week of cruising around the ocean is turning out to be far, far more stressful than it really should be.

After I press send, I avoid Holly and Dad as best I can for a full twenty-four hours, telling them I'm not feeling a hundred percent, and hole up in the cabin. And then I wait, checking my emails several times a day. Right now, I need the kind of comforting words only a best friend can give.

FROM: "Alexa Milton" <alexainexile@mymail.com>
TO: "NJM" <toohottohandle@mymail.com>
SUBJECT: Oh, Nessa...

I don't know what to say. Nessa's Lessons in Love? Oh, Nessa. I know if I say what I want to say you're not going to like it, but here it goes anyway...

Be careful. You're messing with people's lives here. People you don't know very well. It's just that...well, you know how things get with your Marilynisms, don't you? And you know I think you're a complete scream and I wouldn't change you for anything, but sometimes...hmmm… how can I say this? Okay, straight to the point: you get a bit excited about it all and things don't turn out so good. How do you really know that Ted's right for Holly? You've only spoken to him a few times. Try to stop and think about what you're doing. Make sure you're doing the right thing for everyone, won't you? Oh, and the lying about your age thing—is that really the best idea? I know I sound like I'm nagging and I don't want to sound like that, I truly don't. I'm just worried about you. Especially because I'm not there.

Look, I've got to go. I'm not supposed to be emailing as it is. Please, Ness, be careful. Don't get yourself into any trouble.

Alexa( )( )( )

Oh.
I really do feel like crying when I read this. Comforting words? Not likely. So much for best friends. So much for any friends. Because I don't seem to have any at the moment. I sniff, and then, just as the tears are starting to well over, the cabin door opens, and my dad comes into the room. He wanders about for a bit, sorting through some papers on his bed, and I try to distract myself from crying by snapping Sugar Kane shut.
"Oh, hi, sweetheart. I didn't notice you there."
Didn't notice me. In here? Is that even possible?
He must have found what he's looking for, because he straightens up and comes over to plant a kiss on the top of my head. "Must dash. I just forgot a few papers. I won't be back until dinner."
And then he's gone.
I really do cry then.
No best friend. No friends. Not even any Dad.

Wow. Not even any Dad...Things really are bleak.

I spend the time until dinner trying to calm myself down and taking stock. Maybe my run-ins with Marc and mini-fight with Alexa are just making me over-dramatize things? After all, everything else is going pretty well. Holly and I worked out the Nessa's Lessons in Love thing. And she looks happier for it. As if a weight's been taken off her shoulders. That's good. She doesn't have much time for Dad's study, with all her dates. That's good as well. Really, I should try to be more positive—Holly and Ted have spoken a number of times now, and the other day, I even caught them having a laugh about something. So, that's good as well, isn't it? That's progress and—

Oh. The phone's ringing.

I pick it up. "Hello?" I say hesitantly. Wondering if it's Marc.

"Hey, Nessa. How're you feeling?" It's Holly.

Phew. And it doesn't sound like Marc's told her about the Ted thing. Double phew. "Um, good. I think. Better."

"Great!"

"What've you been up to?" Please say you've been spending time with Ted, please say you've been spending time with Ted, I send up a silent prayer.

"Um, this and that. I've been spending quite a bit of time with Antonio today, actually."

Oh.

"There's some kind of crazy '80s disco on tonight. We're going to that. Want to come?"

No, I think, but then I remember: be positive. Maybe I can use this as an opportunity to get Holly and Ted together again. To get them to see each other outside of their usual roles. To get those eyes to meet across the crowded dance floor. "Okay," I say. "That would be great."

"Fantastic!" Holly replies. "I'll see you up there at eight. And don't forget to dress '80s!"

Eleven

That evening, Dad and I have dinner and head back to our cabin. Within minutes, he's sorting through some more papers (he leads such an exciting life—dinner and then other people's sex lives). I flick on the TV and throw myself down onto the bed.

"I've got quite a few interviews to do tonight. Will you be okay watching TV?"

"Um, sure." I'd been ready to argue long and hard about why I should be allowed to go to the disco, but maybe I won't need to do much arguing at all. Fine by me! He plants another kiss on the top of my head (seriously, I'll be getting a bald patch to match his soon) and is gone.

It takes me a good half-hour to sort out something '80s, including begging a steward for a pair of white cotton gloves and snipping the fingers off (I knew I should have bought a bedazzler during the recent '80s revival). And after a lot of eyeliner and hair-teasing and spending a good five minutes piling all my jewelry on, I'm ready to go. The clothes aren't great—just plain and black—but it's all I can do with such short notice. I'll have to remember that the next time I go cruising, an extra suitcase full of costumes will be mandatory.

Before I head off, I leave a note for my dad saying I'm hungry and have gone for a "midnight snack"...at 8.15 p.m.. Still, after the way I've been eating on this trip, Dad's sure to buy it.

"Hey, Nessa!" Holly calls out from the dance floor. "Over here!"

I blink hard, trying to get a good look at her, the strobe lights making it difficult, but then they stop. And I practically lose it when I see her. Her outfit is amazing. "Where on earth did you get a bubble skirt?" Not only because she's wearing a bubble skirt, but because she actually looks *good* in it. How can anyone look good in a bubble skirt? Honestly, she should be arrested.

"I saw some girl wearing one the other day, tracked her down, and paid her a hundred bucks for it. Thank goodness for that recent '80s revival."

"I was just thinking the same thing before. But a hundred bucks?! You're crazy," I laugh.

"It was worth it to see her out of that bubble skirt." Holly shudders. "It was *not* a good look."

"Where's Antonio?" My eyes search the dance floor.

Holly shrugs. "He was supposed to meet me an hour ago for dinner, but he just never showed up."

My mouth falls open. "He stood you up?"

Holly laughs. "Don't look so shocked. It's happened before."

Hmmm. Holly looks a bit too jolly for my liking. And I remember what Marc said that first night at dinner: *If she hides her feelings, it's easier for her.* "Holly..." I start, giving her a look. Sometimes that girl is a bit of a worry.

But she waves a hand. "No, really. I mean it. Antonio's a lovely guy, but he's not the guy for me. He's been a nice...diversion, though."

Oh. I thought she was just trying to make light of the whole Antonio thing, but I can see from her expression that she's not at all. And then, just as I'm thinking all of this, Holly grins this amazingly big grin.

"Holly..." I start once more. "Have you met someone?"

Holly shrugs a little shrug and shakes her bubble skirt. "Maybe."

"Who is it?" I grab both her arms.

"Hey, great gloves!" she says, avoiding my question.

"Holly! Tell me!"

"Nope," she says with a laugh. "My lips are sealed. This time, I really, really don't want to jinx it. This time...I think it might even be for real. He's just lovely. Kind and caring and, well, just perfect."

"What? PM? You're kidding!" I'm so excited I want to jump up and down on the spot.

"Maybe. I hope so." Holly smiles. "I just hope he sees me in the same way. I think he does, but I'm not quite sure yet. Anyway, it's all thanks to you."

"Me?" My eyes boggle now.

Holly nods. "Yep. You."

Oh. Oh, wow. It's Ted she's talking about. It just has to be! He's the only guy she's spent a decent amount of time with since the start of the cruise, besides Antonio. I've made sure of that. I take a quick look around, trying to see if Ted's here (of course, I'd called him and told him Holly was going to be here). "So, your mystery man, is he here?"

"I didn't tell him I was coming," Holly says. "I thought we could have a girls' night out."

There's a big pause as I stand, hands on hips, and wonder how I can get any more information out of her. In front of me, Holly keeps grinning her big grin, loving the fact that I'm dying over here.

"Ugh! You're so mean!" I dance up and down again. "Give me just a little something. His initials. The first letter of his name. Something!"

Holly gives her bubble skirt a shake. "Nope."

"HOLLY! You've got to give me something. Anything!"

"Oh, all right then. Maybe his first initial is T." She shakes her skirt again. "Or maybe it isn't."

But I only hear the first part of her sentence. T! T! His first initial is T! It's Ted! It's Ted! It's Ted! I knew I was right. I knew it all along. All those Marilynisms, all those signs. It was meant to be.

Holly grabs my arm, pulling me in next to her. "Now, stop busy-bodying and let's go!"

She drags me out onto the dance floor. It takes me a good song and a half to come down from cloud nine, but when I do, I breathe a sigh of relief. It's a good thing one of us told Ted where she was going to be tonight. It's a good thing I pulled myself out of my funk and came, after all.

Holly and I dance like mad things for an hour or so before stopping for sustenance. Every so often, while we're on the dance floor, that surreal feeling washes over me again, especially when people stare at us. Me. Me and Holly Isles. We're dancing. And laughing. And whooping like mad things. And drinking strange concoctions with 80s names. How can this be happening to me? How can this be real? My brain screams the questions at me over and over again. But whenever these thoughts come into my head, I just have to remember what Holly told me that day at cocktails/mocktails – that being me, Nessa, is the important thing. It doesn't matter that Holly's famous and I'm far from it. I just have to be me. We just have to be each other. Two gals on a dance floor. In the moment. And when I remember this, everything feels more real again and I have such a good time that I forget about the people staring and just go with it.

After a second hour on the dance floor, Holly goes off to the bathroom and I race outside and give Ted's cabin a quick call. He hasn't turned up yet and I'm wondering where he is.

"Ted?" I say when he picks up. "Are you coming to the disco? Holly's here."

"Um, yep. In a few minutes. I'm just filing some photos and I'll be there."

I wince when I hear this. I hope the photos are of another one of the famous people on board the ship (maybe even Antonio) and not Holly. "Okay. See you then." I hang up and race back into the disco again, where I pick us up two more drinks. "Here you go," I say, giving one to Holly when she returns.

"Oh, thanks. I'm dying of thirst." We guzzle them down and hit the dance floor once more.

After another fifteen minutes or so of *Thriller, Girls Just Want to Have Fun,* and *Wake Me Up Before you Go-Go,* Holly signals to me. "Want another drink?" she bends over and yells in my ear.

I shake my head. "You go. I'll stay here."

Holly nods. "Be back in a sec."

I give her the thumbs up. There's no way I'm leaving the dance floor when George Michael's singing. I mean, that would be '80s sacrilege! Anyway, I want to keep an eye out for Ted and—

Ugh. Yuk.

"Well, hello, pretty lady," the guy says, sidling up in front of me. And close. Too close.

"Um, hi." I take a step back. "Nice, um, costume."

He looks down. "What?"

"You know, from the '80s."

"Huh?" He looks down again. And, with this look, I can see, in his world, the black skinny leather tie never went out of fashion. Oh, gross.

He steps forward again, this time even closer.

"Hey!" I say.

"Hay's what horses eat, sweetheart. I recognized you from across the room. You're the little filly with the pop-off top, aren't you?"

Filly? Pop-off top? Yuk. I twist my head, having a quick look in the crowd for Holly. Where is she?

"Why don't we go back to my cabin and you can do your little pop-off act for me?" He gives me a suggestive wink.

I turn and look him straight in the eye now. "You sicko! Do you know how old I am? Thirteen!" I hiss my age at him, not wanting everyone around me to hear. I turn to go, but he moves in even further again and grabs me.

"No, you're not. You wouldn't be in here, if you were."

This doesn't seem to turn him off in the slightest, in fact, his grip tightens. And it's tight now. Really tight. Suddenly all my anger at the guy crumples inside me and a new feeling rushes in: fear. I wish I really was back in the cabin watching TV, like I'm supposed to be. Where's my dad? Where's Holly?

I look around again quickly. No-one's really noticed there's anything untoward going on because the music's so loud. When I turn back and face him again, he leers at me. Right. That's it. "Get lost. Holly!"

I'm scared now. Really scared. And I turn my head and yell hard. A light flashes in my face and my eyes scan the crowd quickly, hoping it's Ted and that he'll come and save me.

"Ted?" I yell. "Ted?" But I can't see him anywhere. Oh, no. I think I'm going to cry again. "Hol –" But before I can get her name out again, the guy's arms get yanked off my hips and he goes flying halfway across the dance floor.

"Didn't you hear her? She said get lost!" a voice yells, and everyone realizes something's going on then and pulls back.

I'm left standing on my own, kind of stunned, in the middle of it all. I can't move. But then I do, because the person who's thrown the guy across the room comes back over to touch me on the arm. I go to jump as his skin touches mine, but strangely, at the last second, I don't. I lean in toward him instead, because suddenly I feel safe again with Marc beside me. He leads me through the crowded disco, and as we leave the room, a security guard asks him if I'm okay and he nods. "Just tell Holly she's with me, will you? She's at the bar."

"Sure," the guy says, and moves off to find her.

It's cold out, and I don't complain when Marc pulls his sweater off and dresses me in it. Telling me to stick my arms up and through, like I'm two years old again. The sea air, though, is good, after the stale air of the disco. So is the cold. I think it helps me to separate myself from what's just gone on inside.

"Nessa, you shouldn't have been in there," Marc says. "You're only sixteen."

I turn and look at him, finally in the moment.

"Are you okay?" Marc continues.

I go to nod and then stop, frozen. Am I okay? I don't know.

"Did you want me to get your dad for you?"

Yes, my head says, but "No" is what comes out of my almost fourteen-year-old mouth (oh, yeah, I feel so grown up right now). The fact is, if my dad ever, ever, ever finds out about this, my life won't be worth living. I'm doubting I'll even be able to tell him when I'm fifty. "No, I'm...fine," I tell Marc. At least I think I'm fine. Or I will be soon. I take a deep breath and look back in the direction of the disco. I shake my head slightly, trying to get a grip on all of this. I can't quite remember how we got out here and everything feels so strange and...

Oh. Hang on a second. Tears. I'm crying, I realize, as tears roll down my face. I can't believe all the crying I've been doing on this trip. "You're right. I know I'm only, um, you know, young," I say. "I know. I wish I hadn't gone at all now." And I try to stop myself, but the tears and the words all fall out, tumbling over each other. "I wish I'd stayed in the cabin and watched TV, and I wish my dad was here, and I wish I could email Alexa and make up, and I wish you weren't angry with me and..." I think I could keep going forever, but I can't because suddenly...

I can't seem to help myself.

My mouth is on Marc's and we're kissing.

I must still be dreaming, the thought crosses my mind. But then I remember yesterday—when I'd thought Marc was going to kiss me—and I feel his lips, finally, on mine and realize I'm not dreaming at all. Marc and I, we're kissing. Actually kissing. It's hard to believe it's truly happening at first. I mean, there's no denying we're a bit on again off again. One minute we're friends and the next minute I do something dumb, like I just did inside the disco, and Marc's angry at me once more, which I can hardly blame him for, but now...wow. We're really kissing.

And it's warm and good and, somehow… right.

I manage to get back to the cabin five-and-a-half minutes before my dad, turn the TV on, chuck the note out and jump in the shower. Within fifteen minutes, I'm tucked up in bed, and after Dad reads for half an hour, it's lights out. But do you think I sleep? No way.

I keep replaying that kiss in my head, over and over and over again. And it's like some kind of drug, because every time I replay it, my heart *boom, boom, boom, boom, booms* so loud I'm sure I'm going to wake Dad up. But I can't help myself. If you'd been kissed like that, you'd replay it in your head, too. Even if you were never kissed again, it'd keep you going until you were old and grey.

And I'm so happy. So, so happy. I think I feel even more happy because of the contrast with this afternoon when I was so miserable and the revolting incident of this evening. It's like this one good thing has cancelled everything else out. Finally, everything's working out perfectly. Holly and Ted. Marc and me.

At ten past midnight, I can't bear it any longer. I have to tell someone (and I'm hardly going to wake up Dad and tell him). So I reach over quietly and grab Sugar Kane from under my bed.

FROM: "NJM" <toohottoohandle@mymail.com>
TO: "Alexa Milton" <alexainexile@mymail.com>
SUBJECT: Three words...

Marc. Kissed. Me.

Nessaxxx

I surf for a few minutes (okay, so I admit it, I even Google Marc's name). I have a hard time following the links that come up, though (nothing exciting—just school awards and stuff), as every time I remember that kiss, my fingers shake, making it hard to press the right buttons. Wow. My fingers are really shaking. It must've been a good kiss. In fact, it was so good—I glance over at my dad, whose breathing has just changed, no, it's okay, he's still asleep—it was just like the movies. Like that bit in *Gentlemen Prefer Blondes* when Lorelei kisses Gus, and he forgets everything he'd been saying and almost falls over, and Dorothy asks Lorelei if she puts Novocaine in her lipstick. Except it would have been Marc with the Novocaine in his lipstick, and I don't think Marc wears lipstick, and wait, this is getting a bit weird, but...Oh. There's an email for me...

FROM: "Alexa Milton" <alexainexile@mymail.com>
TO: "NJM" <toohottohandle@mymail.com>
SUBJECT: Again, what? What?!

I knew it! I knew something was going to happen. I told you to give me frequent Marc updates. And what do I get? Nothing. Nothing. Now give me details. All the details. I'm begging you. Or I may have to package myself up and FedEx myself out of here and onto the ship.

Oh, and Nessa Joanne Mulholland, you ignored my last email.

Not very nice.

I'd like a response on what you've been up to. And soonish. Someone needs to keep an eye on you. Your dad, I know, is mid-study, so you're probably getting away with a whole lot more than you should be.

Alexa( )( )( )

Alexa's final comments are a complete downer, and on reading them, I immediately snap Sugar Kane shut with a frown.

I'm on such a high, I don't want to think about anything bad tonight. Right now, life's perfect, and I don't want to be lectured or frowned at or "spoken to" or anything like that. All I want to do is remember that kiss...ah.

I lean back over again and push Sugar Kane under the bed once more. As I do, I see the time on the bedside clock, which reminds me it's tomorrow and the word "tomorrow" makes me think about what's going to happen in the morning—when I see Marc. Because that makes me think that he's going to want to talk. Yes, maybe he'll want to talk about "the kiss" (and wouldn't I be fine with a replay!) but he's also going to want to talk about what happened at the disco and about our fight the other day. And that's one thing I really don't want to talk about—our fight the other day.

I hate that Ted's filing stories on Holly, but I've got to keep those romantic rendezvous coming because I've got to get them to fall even deeper in love so I can be sure they'll do the whole perfect wedding, perfect house, perfect babies thing. I mean, sometimes love needs a helping hand (and this helping hand will be disembarking in France). And I know Marc doesn't like the fact that Ted keeps turning up absolutely everywhere, but he'll be happy when Holly's happy and everything's perfect, perfect, perfect and we have our double wedding just like at the end of *Gentlemen Prefer Blondes*—Holly and Ted and me and...

Oops, that would be illegal at my age, wouldn't it? Well, Holly and Ted can get married, and Marc and I will, um...gaze at each other soulfully or something. (That's if my dad doesn't kill Marc first.)

Yes, I think, settling my head back down onto my pillow dreamily. I'm not going to think about that last bit of Alexa's email. I'm going to pretend that every single last detail in my little world is fitting together. And I'm going to think about that kiss. Over and over again.

Twelve

I've arranged to meet Holly for the special Chocoholics Anonymous afternoon tea at 4 p.m.. I call Ted a few minutes before I'm due at the restaurant.

"So, are you coming?" I ask.

"Wouldn't miss this one for the world."

Sure, I think, my eyes narrowing slightly. And last night, would he have missed an opportunity to photograph Holly Isles getting down and dirty on the dance floor? Was that flash I saw, mid-sleaze moment, from Ted's camera perhaps? Hmmm...

Almost immediately I dismiss the thought—come on, we're talking PM here! Perfect Man! Anyway, I realize I'll have to be a little more careful in the future. Especially where disgusting drunken disco guys are concerned. I shudder thinking about it again, and with a shake of my head, return my thoughts to the plan. I decide to go for broke. "Holly's amazing, isn't she?"

"I wouldn't photograph anyone else. She's just beautiful. Not just on the outside, either."

Wow. This cheers me up. After all, what Ted's just said—it's a bit of a compliment, isn't it? "Um, have you had a chance to chat to her much lately? In the last few days, I mean?"

On the other end of the line, Ted pauses. "Chat?"

"Yes, chat."

"Er, a bit, I guess."

That's something at least. "And how are you getting along?"

Another pause. "Great, I suppose. Holly and I always get along just fine. She's given me some great photo-opportunities this trip."

Oh. Photo-opportunities weren't exactly what I had in mind. I was thinking more along the lines of great kisses. Kind of like the great kiss I had last night. Mmmmm...

"You still there?"

Oops. "Sorry. I was just thinking about something."

"Well, I've got to go. I'll see you there. Bye."

I hang up the phone, apply a little more lip-gloss and head upstairs. Wondering, as I go, about how I can get Ted to see Holly less as a subject to photograph and more as a subject to embrace. I've got to get him thinking about her the way she's thinking about him. Like Holly said, *I just hope he sees me in the same way. I think he does, but I'm not quite sure yet.* Hmmm. Tricky.

I press the button for the elevator with a shake of my head. This love thing—it's not easy. And it seems to get even less easy the older people get. It's like they grow blinkers as they age and can only see straight ahead. They have this defined image of what someone they might be interested in will be like and if anyone's slightly different, they don't see them at all.

It was like that with Jessica and my dad. She was always buying him clothes with labels. The kind of labels she wanted him to wear and that my dad had never heard of. He's more a jeans and tweed blazer kind of guy (yes, the kind with the patches on the elbows—a complete college-professor-geek fashion story). He looked silly in the clothes, though he'd wear them when Jessica was around (and scratched at his collar uncomfortably every five seconds). I never got it.

They would have been quite happy together if she'd just let him wear what he wanted. All I could see was that Jessica had this image of what her partner should wear and she was going to make my dad fit that mold. Stupid, really. And it wasn't because of the clothes that they broke up, it was because of what the clothes meant—that she was trying to change him. And he didn't want to change. (Surprisingly, despite his whole sad Dad thing, I didn't, and still don't want him to change either.) Hmmm. I have to figure out a way to get those Ted blinkers off. And fast.

The elevator doors ping open, and I step out, my heart starting up that familiar *boom, boom, boom, boom, boom*, because the first thing I see is Marc. Marc and Holly.

Oh. But wait. Oh, no. Marc. Marc's there. Not sure what to say to him, I try to back into the elevator, but it's too late. They've seen me. Both of them. And, *whump*, with one last step back, my butt hits the just-closed elevator doors.

Marc and Holly race over. "Are you okay?" Holly asks.

I take a quick step forward. "Of course I am. Me and these elevators. Ha ha. They seem to have it in for me. It was just that...um, I forgot something, and I, um, was going to go back and get it, you see."

"Oh," Holly says. "What did you forget?"

What did I forget? My mind goes blank. Think of an excuse, Nessa. A good one. And quickly. "Um, er...lip-gloss. I forgot my lip-gloss."

"Easy!" Holly reaches into her pocket, pulls out a tube of lip-gloss, and hands it to me.

"Um, thanks," I say, squeezing some out and applying it. Now what am I going to do? I finish applying and pass it back over.

The three of us stand and look at each other.

"Hi," Marc says eventually, taking a step toward me.

"Um, hi," I say.

He takes another step forward. Oh no. I look up just as his face closes in on mine and freak out. What's he doing? He wants to kiss me here? Now? Oh, hang on, he wants to kiss me on the cheek. Like a friend. I move my head at the last moment and we end up kissing on the lips. Oh, no...

Marc pulls back.

There's an awkward silence.

And then Holly whistles. "Well, well, well."

Both Marc and I give Holly a dirty look.

"Well, well, well..." She whistles again.

"Cut it out," Marc tells her.

"I, um, didn't know you were coming," I say to him.

"I didn't know it was a Chocoholics Anonymous afternoon tea. But as I haven't been to a meeting in a while, I thought I'd better come along."

"You like chocolate?" I'm surprised. I mean, not that it's weird or you have to be insane or something to like chocolate (if it is, I should be locked up), but it's usually a girl thing, right? I glance over at the half-filled tables. I don't think there's another guy in here.

"I'm a dark chocolate fan. The darker the better."

Holly makes a face. "You should see what he eats. The really expensive bitter stuff. I can't bear it."

Marc nods. "Which is a good thing, because I can buy it and it lasts for more than five minutes in the pantry."

"Are you suggesting I'd eat it?" Holly says. "You know I can't eat chocolate. Russell doesn't let me eat chocolate."

Marc snorts. "Yes, that's why you're here. At the Chocoholics Anonymous afternoon tea. Russell's her personal trainer," he says to me, before turning back to Holly. "And Russell obviously doesn't live in our pantry."

I'd laugh, but I'm too busy freaking out. Not about the misplaced kiss (embarrassing though it was and I'm sure I'll freak out about it later), but about Ted. Because now I have to stop Ted from turning up. Marc will probably explode if he sees him here and anything between us will be off again. Tucked away in the restaurant, for Ted just to turn up—it's too much of a coincidence on such a big ship. He couldn't just be passing by and happen to see us. Maybe I could get him to smear his face with chocolate or something and pretend he's a closet chocoholic? I groan. No, that's too stupid.

"Um, Nessa?" Marc looks back, and I see that he and Holly are halfway across the room, heading toward the already set-up tables.

Wow, I really have to stop spacing out. "Sorry!" I say and jog over to catch up.

♨

"What's the matter, Nessa?" Holly says, picking up her third miniature chocolate éclair. She inspects it with a frown, as if it's done the wrong thing and needs to be punished. "Now, this is really the last one. I mean it."

"Huh?" I put my cake fork down.

"You've been toying with that piece of sacher torte for the last fifteen minutes. You're putting our table to shame. If you don't like it, try something else. I can personally vouch for the éclairs. All of them."

Toying with my sacher torte? That's not like me. I look down. Oh, I guess I have been. My eyes flick past Marc and over to the elevators again. For about the five-hundredth time.

Marc's eyes move to the elevators as well. "Are you looking for your dad? Is he coming after all?" he asks.

"Mmmfff. Yummy. Is he coming?" Holly pops the rest of the éclair in her mouth. "He said he couldn't make it."

"You invited my dad?" I forget about the elevators for a second.

Holly nods, licking her fingers one by one. "Mmmm. Maybe I could just have a little taste of...what? Sorry. Um, yes. I was having a chat with him yesterday."

"For a couple of hours..." Marc starts, and I whip my head over to look at him. What? "And a couple of hours the day before. Pretty much every day, in fact." Double what?

"You..." Holly replies, and I whip my head back to see her give him a warning look.

"Yes?" Marc says, and I whip my head back again. Ow. This Wimbledon-like conversation is starting to hurt. But what's going on here? Holly's been spending hours with my dad. Every day. All the time we've been on the ship. And how come I don't know about this? How much did I miss while I was being miserable? Marc can't mean Holly's been spending hours with my dad *literally*. He probably means Holly chatted to him for a few minutes once and it *felt* like hours, or even days (this is far more believable). Oh, no. Unless she really is participating in Dad's study now as one of his subjects? And I don't think Holly wants me to, but I have to ask.

"You've been spending hours with my dad?" I look over at her once more.

"Um, it's a pity I can't be part of his study." Holly's eyes move away from mine, obviously avoiding the question. "I think it's really interesting."

Phew. Holly can't be part of the study. That's good news. And I'm about to call her on the avoiding-the-question thing when the elevator doors open. I can't help it. My eyes automatically flick over at the sound. And it's just as I feared. Across the room, our eyes meet. Go away! Get out of here! I try to send him subliminal messages. But it doesn't work. He looks away quickly (he's not supposed to acknowledge me, after all) and makes a break for it, trying to duck behind one of the potted palms.

Too late.

"Oh, goody," Holly says, swiping another éclair. "It's Ted. And his camera."

I stop breathing. My eyes flick over to Marc's face. He's already staring at me. Really staring, with cold, hard eyes.

And that's when I realize this is the end of the line. Marc knows for sure that I've been tipping Ted off. There's no point in denying it like the other day, there's no point in saying anything. And because there's no point in denying what's going on, this time, I don't look away. I stare right back. And it's not in defiance. I'm not sure what it is. I just can't seem to stop looking at him. I can't tear my eyes away from his.

"Sometimes I wonder if Ted has a homing device on me," Holly says, from somewhere far, far away. "Now, that's most definitely my last éclair. I might head off, actually. I promised I'd meet someone later. You kids have fun. But not too much fun. Don't think I didn't see that kiss before..."

I look up then, realizing that Holly's talking. Saying something about leaving. "I might, um, go too," I say to Holly's retreating figure, and scramble out of my chair.

"Not so fast." Marc grabs my arm, pulling me back down. But not before I see Holly and Ted leave the restaurant and get in the elevator together. Oh, brilliant! Maybe they'll go get a coffee or something! I'm almost happy for a second—until I feel Marc's hand on my arm again.

"You look pretty pleased with yourself." He's still staring at me.

Back to reality. "Me?"

"Oh, don't play dumb, Nessa. You're not. And I've really had enough of it now. I'm sure Ted got a few good shots of Holly stuffing her face. That's what you wanted, wasn't it?"

I don't say anything. But something is telling me we're definitely off again.

"I knew it." Marc shakes his head. "I knew you were tipping him off all along. I was just too...too stupid to believe it. Too blind. You're good, I'll give you that much. You're really good. It's clever. A good cover. Which tabloid are you with, anyway? And how old are you really? Eighteen? Nineteen? I'm betting you're something like one of those really young-looking journalists who go back to high school and report on the whole experience. I should have known. And what's going on with your father, as well? Pushing himself on Holly. That's if he really is your father..."

Huh? It takes a while for what he's saying to sink in. And then, to quote Alexa, What? What?! Marc thinks I'm with a tabloid? That I'm nineteen? That my dad isn't my dad? What?! And, if this is what he thinks, why was he kissing me last night?

But, again, like before, I can't say anything. I'm frozen. My body, my eyes—frozen. I can't move, can't talk. Nothing. It's because of his eyes, I realize. I've met Marc's eyes again and I'm transfixed—because they're saying a lot more than his mouth is saying. And I have to admit that looking into them is one of the most painful things I think I've ever done, because I see all kinds of things I never wanted to see in a friend, especially Marc: hurt, pain, confusion, betrayal.

"Well? Are you going to say anything? Defend yourself? Make me look like a complete idiot for trusting you for as long as I have?"

Nothing. Frozen.

Marc snorts. "I can't believe I..." He shakes his head, throws his napkin onto the table, and pushes back his chair in one fluid movement. "Don't call us," he says. "Either of us. Don't talk to us, don't come near us, don't contact us in any way. Nothing. You or your so-called father."

I hole up in the cabin again, nursing my wounds. I've been thrown off my emotional roller-coaster this time—first so happy, then so depressed, then so happy again, and now I'm..."non-operational" is the only word I can think of. This is beyond depressed. For some distraction, I thinking about going online, then remember Alexa and her email, and I just know she'll have emailed again, so I don't. I try to read a book, but can't concentrate. In the end, I lie back and stare at the ceiling, replaying my confrontation with Marc over and over and over again in my head.

"Hello, pumpkin," Dad says, making me jump. I'd been so caught up in my thoughts that I hadn't even heard him come in the room.

"Oh, hi, Dad." I sit up a bit. He goes over and sits down on his bed, looking a bit glum. "What's up?" I ask.

"Hmmm? Oh, nothing."

You've got to love the guy—he's so transparent. I sit up a bit further. "Yes there is. Come on, tell me."

"It's silly, really."

"Come *on*."

"Er, I was supposed to meet up with Holly late this afternoon. She said she wanted to see some of the data from the study. But about an hour before we were meant to meet, her nephew—Marc, is it?"

Don't remind me. I nod, trying not to wince.

"Well, he called and said that she was busy. I guess..." He pauses for a moment.

"What?"

He shrugs. "I guess she wasn't really interested in the study after all. Perhaps she was just making conversation. It's funny because I thought..." Another pause.

Oh, no. I knew it. I *knew* my dad liked Holly. She hadn't even needed to put her Nessa's Lessons in Love moves on him for it to happen. "You thought what?" He's past glum now. He looks...sad. Despondent even. Just like me. What a pair.

"I thought..." But then he looks up, making an obvious and over-the-top effort to brighten his expression. "Sorry, sweetheart. Like I said, I'm just being silly. Anyway, I've got to get going. I've got another two interviews to do this afternoon." He jumps up from his bed then.

I sit up properly now. "But, Dad..."

"No," he says, waving one hand as he opens the cabin door with the other. "Don't you worry about me. I'll see you in a few hours. We'll have a lovely dinner. Just the two of us. All right?"

I nod. And then he's gone. But I can't help but notice that, just before the door closes (when he thinks I can't see him anymore), his shoulders do that all-too-familiar slump again.

To the sound of his retreating footsteps, I fall back down on the bed. That's my fault, those slumped shoulders. All my fault. I've hurt everyone around me, including myself. My dad, who now thinks that Holly isn't really interested in him or his study; Marc, who thinks I'm some kind of tabloid journalist hanging around with a guy who isn't my father (who's he supposed to be, anyway, my editor?); Holly, who's going to think Dad and I are ignoring her; and Alexa, who I know for sure thinks I'm ignoring her.

Just for a second, all of this makes me question whether I'm doing the right thing—trying to get Holly and Ted together. But just for a second. No longer. Because it has to be right, doesn't it?

Like I've been thinking all along, it's too perfect. Holly herself had said she thought she'd met PM. PM whose first initial was T. Yes. Even if I don't know what I have to do next, I have to keep believing that it's the right thing to do. I have to have faith. In Holly. And Ted. And in Marilyn. I know that it will all work out in the end. It always does. Just like in the movies. Like they say, it's darkest before dawn. And that's always true in the movies—things always get very, very complicated before they unravel and work themselves out. And this is the complicated bit. Ugh, the really complicated bit.

I just wish I knew how to make it all work out.

Double ugh. I turn over and put my head under the pillow. I want this trip to be over.

Yesterday.

bm

As it turns out, though, Dad and I don't have dinner alone. Instead, we get invited to have dinner at the Captain's table. I don't think either of us really wants to go, not feeling much like socializing, but apparently being asked to dine at the Captain's table is a Big Deal, so we don our finest and head up to the restaurant like the good little passengers that we are.

And I wish I was feeling more up to this, because the Captain is a complete and utter darling, and the people on the table turn out to be really interesting—there's a guy who used to be a cosmonaut, a ballerina, a political activist who makes documentaries, Dad, and um, me (hey, not that I feel out of place or anything!). In a way, it makes me kind of proud of my dad. That people think he's interesting and what he does is important, even if he doesn't make much money doing it, like Holly or Antonio.

I'm chatting to the ex-cosmonaut (who's got the best accent!) and am even starting to enjoy myself a tad when I see them.

Marc and Holly.

Oh, no. Of course, I panicked when Dad said we were going to the proper restaurant. And I almost lost the plot when I saw we were going to be sitting at table one, right near table three—Holly's table. But then no-one had appeared, and I thought I was safe. That they were ordering dinner in their suite or something.

Wrong.

As they make their way to their seats, I focus my full attention back on Nikolai, the ex-cosmonaut. Well, my full attention except for one eye, which keeps a tab on what's going on at the next table. Hang on, is that...?

It is! Antonio. Oh, no. Antonio sits down beside Holly.

Now I can't help myself. I really do look over. Seeing my movement, Holly glances over and waves. She goes to get up, but Marc reaches up and touches her arm. Says something to her. She glances down at him, then over at me for a second, then at my dad for even longer. Finally, a puzzled look comes over her face before she sits back down once more. And, in that moment, I know it wasn't Holly's idea to cancel her appointment with my dad this afternoon. It was Marc's. She doesn't know anything about it. And who knows what he's told her about us? Both this afternoon and just now.

Holly doesn't look at me, or my dad, again all evening. As for Marc, he never even looks at me at all.

Antonio, however, does enough "looking" for everyone. He doesn't take his eyes off Holly all night long. In fact, he's all over her. The weird thing is that, at first, it looks like he's annoying Holly. But as the night progresses, she seems to change her mind. And by the time our main courses are taken away, strangely, Nessa's Lessons in Love get dusted off and brought out once more. Holly starts flirting and simpering and batting her eyelashes, to the point where I kind of wish I'd never given her any lessons at all. Even more strangely, even though Holly's doing all of this, she doesn't look like she's having a good time. I can't help noticing that my dad's eyes flick over to table three involuntarily, watching them, Holly and Antonio, all too often. He can't help himself, poor guy. I feel a stab in my heart then. Dad must really like Holly. So, for him to watch this...ugh, it must just be awful. Far, far more awful than it is for me.

As we work our way through dessert and coffee, Antonio just gets worse. Louder and more over the top. He's so not right for Holly, and while she was trying before, now she really doesn't look like she's enjoying herself. But she doesn't tell Antonio to go away, either. Beside them, Marc looks like he'd rather be anywhere else on Earth than on table three (well, except maybe next to me at table one).

Eventually, as the night wears on painfully slowly, my dad stops looking over at Holly. Which is bad. Because I can tell from his expression that he's now cut her off. He's changed his mind about her. While he might have been disappointed not to see her this afternoon, she's been re-categorized. He's put her back in the "West Coast" box.

Holly's just proved his theory to him. Now, he thinks she's shallow.

Shallow and flighty. And I want to turn to him and tell him she's not. That Holly's not like that. That she's just gone a little crazy in her hunt for PM and doesn't trust any of her actions or reactions anymore. That she's confused and hurt. And most of this is my fault. But what can I say? How can I prove it? Sitting over there, letting Antonio make her look like a fool, how can I tell my dad that Holly's not like that? He wouldn't believe me whatever I said. However I explained it to him.

A little while later, I give up looking at table three as well. It's just...embarrassing. That is, I give up looking until I can't ignore the feeling any longer—the feeling that someone's now looking at me. Staring at *me*. I glance up, my eyes instantly meeting Marc's and my breath catches, tightening in my chest. Quickly, I look away again.

But Marc doesn't.

I can feel his eyes boring into me for the rest of the evening. And every time I can't help myself and take a quick glance over, his eyes are still there, unblinking, unfailing. Staring at me. It's like he's changed his mind and decided that as much as he wants to ignore me, he can't afford to. That he shouldn't let me out of his sight for a second. I can't breathe every time I see this. It's like he's suffocating me. And maybe my dad feels the same way, because he refuses a second cup of coffee (he *always* has a second cup of coffee) and it's not long before he turns to me. "Ready to go, pumpkin?"

Silently, I nod.

We say our goodbyes and then make our way to the elevators.

Marc's eyes don't leave me for a second. I can feel his gaze right up until the elevator doors close.

Dad and I then trudge, again silently, all the way back to our cabin. I think we're both too tired and depressed to try to cheer each other up.

Inside, I sit down on my bed and my dad plants a kiss on that familiar old spot on top of my head. "I'm going to take a quick shower," he says, then grabs a few bits and pieces, makes his way into the bathroom, and shuts the door behind him.

I stare at the bathroom door for what feels like a long, long time and then sigh a long sigh. So, now what? I'm so stuck. I don't know what to do. I can't stay holed up in the cabin for the rest of the trip. For two whole days. That would be stupid. And I can't leave things as they are either. Everyone's so unhappy. I have to do something. I have to make everything right again. I've got two days. Two days to fix everything.

But what am I going to do?

I stare and stare and stare and think and think and think.

And what I come up with is this: I need to stick to the plan. I mean, when in doubt, stick to the plan, right? After all, that's what plans are for. You make them so that when things get tough, you've got something to guide you. To remind you what you have to do. And the plan was, and is, that I have to get Holly and Ted together. To make them see that they're perfect for one another.

Hmmm.

Again, just for a second, I question whether I'm doing the right thing. I think about Marc. And about Alexa and her email. And my gut. But no. I can't think about those things. Because I know I'm right. I think.

Remember, Nessa, it's darkest before dawn. This is the complicated bit. It'll all work out in the end. And once I get Holly and Ted together and everyone's happy and can see that I was right all along, they'll all pat me on the back. And thank me. Won't they?

Again, just for a second, I pause, my eyes on the bathroom door, remembering how unhappy my dad was tonight.

Stop it, Nessa. Just stop it.

Right. That's it. Time to get serious. None of this turning up at the same place at the same time rubbish anymore. I need a cracker of an idea to get Holly and Ted together. Once and for all.

hm

Again, I don't think I sleep at all. And I don't think my dad does either, because he tosses and turns in his bed all night, each toss, each turn, making me feel more awful. Making me more anxious to make things right.

It isn't until almost dawn that I work it out. (And the only reason I know it's almost dawn is because of the red numbers on the alarm clock—there's still not much of a view down here below sea level.) And when I do, it seems so simple. All I have to do is keep following the plot of *Gentlemen Prefer Blondes*. I mean, that's what all the signs have been pointing to all along: the cruise ship, Holly replying to my line when we were boarding, her need to find a decent guy, Ted turning up, the talent quest song...everything. So many signs! So many Marilynisms! And I'm not quite sure how I'm going to do this yet—follow the plot, that is. But it's the faith thing again. It'll come to me. I just need to have faith that I'll get there. That it'll all work out in the end. Just like it does in the movie. After all, it's only in the final few minutes of *Gentlemen Prefer Blondes* that things become clear. And I have two more whole days up my sleeve.

Thirteen

I hide out in the corridor for an hour and a half, until Marc leaves the suite. And I'm tired and I'm hungry, but I wait. Because I need to see Holly, to tell her everything's still okay with us. It was weird, what happened last night at dinner, and I need to talk to her about it. Anyway, there is no way that's going to happen while Marc's on duty, I know. So I wait.

As soon as I see him round the corner, I rush up to her door and knock.

"Oh. Nessa." Holly opens the door only to give me a strange look.

"Hi, Holly."

"Are you really supposed to be here?"

I give her a strange look in return.

"It's just that Marc mentioned your dad thought we were spending a little too much time together."

I pause a second, but then shake my head. "He never said that."

"But..." She frowns, then quickly sighs. "Oh, I see. That Marc. I'm sorry, Nessa. He can be a bit too over-protective at times. He likes to scare off new people."

I snort. "I've noticed."

"Come in, come in." Holly waves me inside. "Believe me, I'll be talking to him later."

I make my way inside, trying not to breathe a too-obvious sigh of relief. At least Marc hasn't told Holly about his weird tabloid journalist theory. Holly shuts the door behind us.

"You know, I called your dad a while ago to apologize for anything I'd done, but he wasn't there. I had to leave a message."

"Oh."

"Can you get him to give me a call when you see him?"

Standing awkwardly in the middle of the room, I can't quite meet her eyes. "Sure," I say, but I realize there's no point. Dad's not going to call Holly back. Not after last night.

Silence.

"Look, I..." Holly starts, but her voice quickly wavers.

I take a step forward towards her. "What's the matter?"

"Oh..." She waves a hand. "I just feel like an idiot. About last night. With Antonio. I don't know why...what I was doing...and now..."

I think back again to the scene at the restaurant. To Antonio and Holly. And her flirting.

"Everything's just so...I can't explain it. I don't know what's wrong with me. I'm so mixed up. I feel like I'm twelve years old again and—" She breaks off as there's a knock on the door.

I almost hit my head on the ceiling, I jump so high. "Who's that?" I say quickly. Please let it not be Marc...

But Holly just waves a hand again. "I called for a steward. I need to send this note to Antonio. I can't seem to contact him and..." She's almost at the door when the phone rings and she hesitates.

"I'll get the door. You get the phone," I say, rushing over to the door. There's no way I'm getting the phone. It could be Marc.

"Thanks," Holly says, abandoning the door and making her way over to the phone instead. She passes me the note as she goes. And I don't mean to read it, but she hands it to me face up. And there are only a few words on it. I can't help it, really. This is what it says:

Can you meet me in my suite—5.30 p.m.?
Love, Holly

Well, I guess it's all still on with Antonio. I open the door for the steward and go to hand him the note, but Holly speaks up just as I'm passing it to him. "Hang on, it's okay. Don't bother with the note—it's Antonio on the phone. Sorry about that," she says to the steward. "Nessa, can you...?" She glances at her purse, sitting on the side table.

Huh? Oh! A tip. I open up Holly's purse and my eyes boggle at the wad of hundreds and fifties and twenties and tens all stuffed in there. I glance up at the steward.

"She usually gives me twenty," he says.

Now I give him a look. "Yeah, right."

He shrugs.

Behind me, Holly pipes up again. "Twenty would be good. Thanks, Nessa."

My eyes widen. Twenty?! For delivering a note? Or not delivering a note, as things stand. Note to Nessa: Add stewarding to possible career list.

And stick to the upper decks. Silently, I pass him a twenty, and he gives me a wink, closing the door as he goes.

"No, that's fine. It doesn't matter...It's not important. We'll catch up some other time...Thanks, Antonio."

I turn toward her, putting her purse back down on the side table.

"Well, so much for that. He can't make it. Not that it really matters. I only wanted to see him to apologize in person for last night. For acting so strangely. The thing is, I'm not interested in Antonio, I'm...oh, it doesn't matter. I'm tired of thinking about it. Anyway, how awful do I feel, dragging that poor steward up here for nothing?"

I just look at her. I don't think the "poor steward" feels equally awful.

"Right. So, what are we up to this afternoon?" Holly claps her hands together. "Something nice? Cocktails/mocktails?"

I pause for a second, remembering Marc and his parting words to me. I shouldn't even be here, let alone meet up with Holly for cocktails/mocktails. "Oh, I can't. I promised my dad that I'd do something for him." Lie, lie, lie.

"Oh." Holly's face falls a bit. "That's okay, I understand."

"Really?"

Holly nods. "Of course. But remember to ask him to call me when he has a minute, won't you? I really want to talk to him. Maybe he'd even like an early dinner."

Hmmm. I watch her carefully. She's avoiding talking about something again. Maybe it's about Ted? "What were you saying before, about last night and not being interested in Antonio?"

There's another wave of a hand. "Oh, nothing. Really, it's nothing. Don't worry about it."

I ask her again, but the moment has obviously passed. Whatever Holly was going to open up about before, it's been locked away inside her once more to be kept safe and sound.

It's only when I'm halfway back to the cabin that I see the steward again. The one that I tipped. And then I look down and realize I still have Holly's note in my hand. Holly's note to Antonio. But with no name on it. I read it again, just to make sure.

Can you meet me in my suite—5.30 p.m.?
Love, Holly

Finally, I know what I have to do.

"Hey!" I call out and the steward halts in his tracks and turns around. "Wait up. Holly's changed her mind."

Well, it's only another *little* lie. Isn't it? And it's for a good cause...Here's hoping he doesn't expect another twenty to make this delivery.

$$\mathcal{wm}$$

FROM: "Alexa Milton" <alexainexile@mymail.com>
TO: "NJM" <toohottohandle@mymail.com>
SUBJECT: Details?

Come on, Nessa. I'm dying over here. I need details!

Alexa( )( )( )

$$\mathcal{wm}$$

FROM: "Alexa Milton" <alexainexile@mymail.com>
TO: "NJM" <toohottohandle@mymail.com>
SUBJECT: Waiting...

Still waiting. Dying a slow and agonizing death. I hope I never have to rely on you to save me from something (mummies most likely—I think we're going to Egypt next year).

Alexa( )( )( )

$$\mathcal{wm}$$

FROM: "Alexa Milton" <alexainexile@mymail.com>
TO: "NJM" <toohottohandle@mymail.com>
SUBJECT: Not very nice at all

You're just ignoring me, aren't you? Because I said that stuff about being careful. Nessa, sometimes you are not very nice. Not very nice *at all*. You can't just ignore things you don't want to face up to, you know.

Don't come crying to me when this all crashes and burns around you. All right?

Alexa

um

FROM: "Alexa Milton" <alexainexile@mymail.com>
TO: "NJM" <toohottohandle@mymail.com>
SUBJECT: Ignore last email

Okay. I'm sorry. I didn't mean that. I'm just freaking out over here. I don't know what's going on and I'm not there to watch out for you.

Friends? Talk to me? Please?

Alexa( )( )( )

I can't help but read my email. I'm only supposed to be online for a few minutes—checking up a few details on the plot of *Gentlemen Prefer Blondes*—but when the emails pop into the correct mailbox, I see there are four from Alexa, remember that she's probably put her life on the line to send them, and the next thing I know, my email program is maximized across Sugar Kane's small screen and I'm reading away.

I have to smile at the emails, despite some of the things they say. They're so...Alexa. That girl is my conscience. And, you have to hand it to her, most of the time she's right. *Most* of the time. But not that time we thought that her dad was having an affair. (He kind of was, but with a mummy. Still, it was a *female* mummy, so she was sort of right.) She's not right now, either. Still, right or not, I can't leave her hanging like this, so I send her a quick reply to ease her mind.

FROM: "NJM" <toohottohandle@mymail.com>
TO: "Alexa Milton" <alexainexile@mymail.com>
SUBJECT: Don't worry

Can't stop to chat, but just a quick email to say *don't worry*. I know what I've got to do (finally – for a moment there I was getting a bit worried!) and now I've just got to do it. I'll tell you all about it tomorrow. When everything's perfect. And everyone's happy. It'll be great...you'll see!

Nessaxxx

I press send, then, with a snap, Sugar Kane is shut again. Right. What's the
time? What?! Five fifteen?! I jump off my bed, grab my coat, and head for
the door.

Time to see my plan put into action.

Back in my now-familiar hiding spot in the corridor (behind the fire
extinguisher box), I stand (well, crouch) and wait for 5.30 p.m. to roll
around. People kind of look at me as they pass by, then let themselves into
their suites and close the door quickly behind them, not knowing if I'm a
thief wanting to steal their Louis Vuitton suitcases, or a stalker wanting to
stab them with their solid-silver letter openers. I guess I kind of am a stalker
(I don't want to stab anybody with anything, though).

I wait for about ten to fifteen minutes before he shows up. Right on
time, I nod, checking my watch. He knocks on Holly's door, waits, waits a
bit more, then he shrugs, reaches out and tries the handle. Hey! I think,
shouldn't he wait just a little bit longer? But, surprisingly, the door is
unlocked. It opens and—I hold my breath—he enters.

Phew.

So far, so good.

I stand up slowly, my knees not being very forgiving about all the
crouching we've been doing lately. I keep my eyes on the door though, still
half-holding my breath as I wait, and lean against the wall.

As each minute passes, I smile a little more. A little wider. My plan—it
seems to be working. I mean, I thought it would, I tried to have faith,
but...well, you never know, do you? I check my watch again. Five minutes.
Six minutes. I watch the second hand tick over. Seven minutes! Seven
whole minutes. I shake my head and start to wonder what's going on in
there. Well, I can guess. Champagne. Oysters. Just like I'd ordered. Then
they'll look at each other and—What?!

Quickly, I crouch down again, my dream scenario fading suddenly.

What's my dad doing here?

He shouldn't be up here. What's he doing? Interviewing someone?
What?

I look again, harder, in case my eyes are deceiving me. But no, there's no mistake. There he is, starting down the corridor. Heading right toward Holly's suite. My eyes widen in fright. And again, just like before, I hold my breath. Which is hard, at the rate my heart's beating now.

He keeps going. Keeps heading toward Holly's suite. Oh, no. He's not interviewing someone—I remember Holly's words then. From this afternoon. How she'd been trying to call him. But no, he can't have returned her calls. He can't have changed his mind. I know him. He wouldn't have called her. Not after last night, after what he'd seen. This isn't part of the plan, this isn't in the script, this isn't...Oh, no. No. No, no, no, no, no.

The elevator doors open again, and I watch in horror as someone else exits and starts up the corridor, tracing my father's footsteps.

Marc.

Again, what? How can this be happening? This isn't right. This isn't what's supposed to happen. We've had the complicated bit. This is supposed to be the end of the complications. This is supposed to be where everything works out. The unraveling.

No. No, no, no, no, no.

Marc pauses for a second as he sees my dad in front of him. And then he starts walking again. Faster this time. Trying to catch up.

I'm really not breathing now. I may never breathe again, in fact.

What should I do? What should I do?

I watch the scene unfolding before my eyes as if it's a real film. A real film shot in lurid Technicolor. There's my dad, approaching Holly's door. A few more steps and he'll be there. There's Marc, hot-footing it up behind my dad, who's completely unaware there's anyone behind him. What's going to happen?

"Out!" The voice makes me jump, and I wonder for a second if I've spoken out aloud.

It makes Dad and Marc jump, too. They both stop walking at exactly the same moment and their heads swivel, trying to locate the noise.

"Out! Get out!" the voice screams now. It's Holly, I realize. The voice. It's not me at all—it's Holly. It's Holly and she's...scared.

And it's in that instant, hearing that scared voice call out, that everything comes together, and I realize what I've done. What I'm doing. The past week flashes before my eyes—as if I'm seeing my life, Holly's life, my dad's life, Marc's life—like a movie as well. Like I'm a bystander looking on. Watching. Except this isn't a movie. And I'm not a bystander.

I'm an *actress*. The villain, even.

My mouth drops open in horror.

Because what I've done, there's no escaping it. What I've done is terribly, horribly, awfully wrong. What have I done? Well, I've planted some paparazzo in Holly's room for a start. I've lied to my dad, lied to Holly, lied way, way too much to the guy I like. I've ignored my best friend (who I'm now, um, thinking may have been right after all). I've tried to force Holly onto some guy she's not really all that interested in, otherwise she would've asked him out eons ago. And I've pushed her away from my dad at every opportunity.

I'm an idiot. An *idiot*.

I look down, feeling something rumble. Oh, my gut. Yes, I remember that. I remember lying on my bed, staring at the ceiling and...ignoring my gut. Ignoring Marc's words. Ignoring Alexa's words. If only I'd stopped myself then. How could I be so stupid? How could I have betrayed Holly? That was what she'd said to me on my first visit to her cabin, wasn't it? That she felt like I wouldn't betray her. She *trusted* me.

"GET OUT!" the voice screams once more, and I jump again. Holly! I wake up to myself to see Dad and Marc already pushing open the door to the suite and running inside. Holly! I don't even stop to think what's going to happen when I get in there. When everyone finds out what's going on. What I've been up to.

All I think about now is Holly.

Holly needs me.

Fourteen

I race into the suite, not stopping until I see Holly herself. She's standing, clinging on to my dad, wrapped up tightly in a bathrobe with ruffled, wet hair. Unbelievable. She must be the only woman in the world who could look good with half a head of shampoo dripping onto her shoulders. Ted is across the room, pushed up against the wall, Marc's finger digging into his chest.

"What do you think you're doing?" Marc yells at him. "Who invited you in here?"

Uh oh. I turn and look at the still open door, wondering if I've got time to make a break for it, now I can see Holly's okay. Probably not. Anyway, I don't think the ship, as big as it is, is big enough to hide out on when everyone finds out what I've been up to.

"Well?" Marc's finger digs in again and now Ted pushes himself up and off the wall and crosses his arms.

"Do you want to calm down? I was *invited*. That's what I think I'm doing here."

Holly clings to my dad a little more. "I certainly didn't invite you." She looks first at Marc, then up at my dad. "I was in the shower..."

"I hope you didn't take any photos of Holly in the shower." Marc crosses his arms, but doesn't move away.

Ted snorts. "Pretty hard without a camera. And if I wasn't invited, what's this?" He pulls something out of his pocket. A piece of paper. He passes it to Marc, who reads it. Then reads it again, frowning. He then gives it to Holly.

"This is your handwriting."

She inspects it, frowning, and then realization slowly dawns. Her eyes flick to mine, looking slightly confused, then at my dad, at Marc and back to Ted. I can tell she's not quite sure what to say. She can't admit, after all, that the note was meant for Antonio. Especially not with my specially ordered oysters–champagne combo sitting over there in the corner, looking like they're just dying to be included in a romantic rendezvous.

"It wasn't meant for you," she says, shaking her head at Ted. "It was meant for...for William." She looks up at Dad. "I thought he might like an early dinner. And I know he loves oysters."

Nice save, Holly. One of my eyebrows raises. She really *is* a good actress.

"Oh, yeah? Is that so? Then how come a steward gave the note to *me*?" Ted sighs, his eyes moving to meet mine.

Double uh oh. Thanks for nothing, Ted.

There's a pause.

And then everyone else's eyes follow Ted's to mine.

Uh oh.

"Nessa Joanne Mulholland," my dad starts. "Did you have something to do with this?"

I try to think of a nice save, like Holly's, but I can't come up with anything fast enough. Anyway, there's something inside me that just wants to come clean. I'm tired of lying, of telling half-truths. I want everything out in the open once and for all. I want a clear conscience. What did I think I was doing? All I want now is for Marc to like me again (if he can), for my dad to be happy (and the way he's holding Holly protectively over there, I think he might already be quite happy—though he may have to let go of her for a bit to give me the lecture of the century, which I know for sure is coming) and I want to be able to talk to Holly like I used to (that is, if she'll talk to me ever again when she finds out what's been going on). I just want that happy ending where everything works itself out. The one I'd thought about so much. And wanted so much I'd been kind of blinded as to what I was doing.

"Nessa Joanne Mulholland?"

"Um." I'm not quite sure what to say. Where to start. In the mirror opposite me, I see myself shrink until I look like I'm about eight years old. "I just thought that...I mean..."

"Yes, Vanessa?" My dad gives me a stern look and I know I'm really in trouble. Vanessa? I haven't heard that for quite a while. Marc frowns, looking at me. But not like he hates me anymore. Now he just looks kind of concerned.

I bite my lip, thinking, then turn to Holly. It's Holly, after all, whom I need to apologize to the most. "I'm really sorry, Holly. It's just that when we got on the boat and you knew that line—from *Gentlemen Prefer Blondes*— and then you needed to find Perfect Man, and Ted was here and he was like

Ernie Malone, well, I started to think that you were a bit like Dorothy and I was a bit like Lorelei and..." I trail off, seeing that absolutely no-one has any idea what I'm talking about. Well, except my dad, that is.

"Nessa Joanne Mulholland!" He steps forward now, closer to me and then groans. "Oh, Nessa. Not this again. I thought we'd put all of this behind us."

Behind my dad, Marc steps forward as well. "Um, I'm sorry, but I don't get it." He looks around, at Ted and then over at Holly. "I don't think any of us do. You're going to have to explain..." His eyebrows are practically meeting in the middle, he looks so confused. Finally, he looks over at my father.

Dad sighs now and turns around, facing Marc, Holly and Ted. "Nessa has a bit of a thing, I guess you could call it, about Marilyn Monroe. She can get a little caught up with it sometimes, for a thirteen-year-old. She has what you'd call an overactive imagination and sometimes she thinks the plots from Marilyn Monroe's films are happening. In real life."

Oh no. I just want to die. There it is. Clear as day. For everyone to see. Not only do I think like I child, now everyone believes I am one, too. Oh, man. I want to spontaneously combust and have my ashes settle into the shag-pile carpet and be vacuumed up by one of the maids and be transported out of the room in a brown paper bag, never to be seen again.

Across the room, Marc is staring at me, kind of white-faced. "Thirteen?" he mouths almost silently, looking first at me, and then at my dad. Something tells me we won't be kissing again.

Ever.

I shrug a small shrug. "Almost fourteen!" I mouth back, then bite my lip. What else can I do?

Silence.

I sneak a peek at Holly. Her face reads confusion as well. "Thirteen, huh? That's, um, younger than I thought...But what's it all got to do with Ted?" she finally asks, glancing over at him.

Good question, I think. Everyone's eyes turn to me again. "Um, in the film, Ernie Malone, he's kind of like a private detective and he takes photos and he falls in love with Dorothy, who I thought was kind of like you," I remind Holly. "And I thought that you might be happy, like Dorothy, if you could just see that Ernie, I mean, Ted, was right for you and..." I trail off again. Now I really *do* want to die. How could I have thought that? I may as well be five, not thirteen. But it seemed so...not logical, but magical at the time. Magical and perfect and right and wonderful—like a movie moment.

Please, someone, institutionalize me, lock me up and throw away the key. I think I've lost it. I'm a danger to society. Who knows who I could try to marry off next?

I've got to explain myself better. Right. Here goes nothing...

"The Nessa's Lessons in Love thing. I mean, I worked out pretty fast that was the wrong way to go. So, I thought that maybe if we followed the plot of the movie properly, you'd meet Perfect Man, like you wanted. And then you said you'd met PM and that his name started with a T—and I thought you meant Ted, because he was just like Ernie Malone and Dorothy fell in love with him even though he wasn't right on the surface, just like Ted wasn't right for you, so I kept trying to get you together because you looked so happy and..." I thought I'd be able to explain myself better, but I can't. Wow. I *really* can't. Waiting to die. Really wanting and waiting to die now...

"Can you explain the Nessa's Lessons in Love thing for me? What's that?" Ted asks and we all turn to see him standing there, pencil and pad in hand, jotting down notes.

"Hey!" Marc leans over and grabs the notebook off him. "Cut that out!"

"So close." Ted snaps his fingers.

Silence again. Around the room, eyes meet and brows crinkle.

But it's Holly who speaks first. "Right. Let's try to clear this up a bit. Now, you thought that Ted and I would be perfect together?" she says.

I nod a tiny nod.

"Oh, Nessa," my dad groans again.

"Ted. And me," Holly says again, unbelievingly.

An even tinier nod from *moi*.

More silence.

But then, in the quiet, there comes this noise from Holly's throat. A gurgle. A chuckle. It grows and swells and she starts laughing, still looking at Ted.

Ted starts laughing, too.

"Ted. And me," she says, once more.

"Holly. And me," Ted says, from across the room.

Oh, great.

Their laughter gets louder and louder as they egg each other on.

"Holly. And me. As if!"

"Ted. And me. Not likely!"

I stand and watch as they laugh so hard I think they're going to be sick. They keep laughing and laughing and laughing until Holly's laughing so hard she's clutching at her sides.

Hey! My mouth hangs open, as Marc and my dad both stare at me and then at Holly and Ted alternately. Hey! Cut it out! I want to say. I'm in trouble here. This is *serious*. And I think that Marc and my dad must see what I'm thinking written all over my face, because Marc starts laughing then as well.

"I thought you were from some tabloid," he says to me, before turning to the others. "I thought she was a *journalist*."

"A journalist?" My dad turns to Marc.

"I thought she was a really young-looking nineteen, not almost fourteen, or thirteen!" Marc says to my dad. "And I thought you were, like, her editor or something!"

"Nineteen? A journalist? Editor?" my dad repeats like a parrot, but then he looks back at Marc again, who's now joining in with the others, laughing himself sick, and he starts up too. "Nineteen? A journalist? Editor?" he laughs along.

Oh, great. Laughing at Nessa disease. I've encountered it before. It's contagious and highly infectious. I stand and watch. And not surprisingly, I'm immune. If only I could be quarantined, maybe for about twenty years. I might have recovered from the embarrassment symptoms by then. Maybe.

In front of me, the laughing continues. For what feels like forever.

All four of them have tears running down their faces now. Only Marc manages to get it together for a second or two to ask me a question. "Let me get this straight," he says. "You thought that all Holly's problems would be solved if you could just get her and Ted together. That's why he's been turning up everywhere?"

I nod that small nod again, feeling more and more stupid by the minute, if that's possible. In the mirror, I see that my face is now beet red. Hey, maybe I *will* spontaneously combust after all.

"And, let me get this straight as well, you thought that this was all like *Gentlemen Prefer Blondes*. Because we're on a cruise ship and Holly recognized some line from the film and because she's been unlucky in love?"

"Hey!" Holly stops laughing for a second, taking the heat off me.

"Well, isn't that true?" Marc looks over at her.

"Yes, but..."

"But, what?" Marc asks.

"But..." Holly pauses and then looks up at my dad, who's by her side again. She smiles up at him. That big, wide smile she's so famous for. "It used to be true. It used to be very true. But I think my luck may have changed..."

From: "NJM" <toohottohandle@mymail.com>
To: "Alexa Milton" <alexainexile@mymail.com>
Subject: Take my life, please

I really will swap you lives. I'd much prefer to be with the dead dusties right now. At least they don't say things like "Hi, Marilyn" or "Hi, Lorelei" every time they see you and then fall about laughing (do they?). Like I explained yesterday, I've never been so embarrassed in my life. Not even when I dyed my hair platinum blonde and it all snapped off and Dad had to take me to get that buzz cut, remember? That was bad, but not this bad.

I'm sorry again for being such an idiot. I should have listened to you. As per usual. I'm cringing again now just thinking about the whole thing – it took Holly, Dad, Marc and Ted the whole rest of the trip to stop laughing. Holly says she thinks she's bruised her lungs from laughing so hard.

Anyway, we're in our little apartment now. In Paris. And have I ever got a few things to tell you. For a start, Marc forgave me almost instantly, because I'm, apparently, just a "complete weirdo". (Okay, so maybe I am.) He even apologized to me for thinking I was taking money from Ted and that I was with a tabloid or something and that my dad wasn't my dad.

Holly forgave me as well. In fact, she thinks the whole thing is an absolute scream and that I should be applauded for having that "overactive imagination" of mine, as my dad calls it. Unfortunately my dad doesn't think quite the same way, but Marc and Holly's reactions have softened the blow a bit, that's for sure. I may not be grounded till I'm 30 after all. But, wait, I haven't told you the big news. The enormous news...

Dad and Holly—they're (pre-)ENGAGED. AGH!

Dad finished up his study and spent the rest of the trip with Holly. And then, as we got off the boat, just as I was wondering what was going to happen with them (well, okay—with Marc and me as well!), Dad stops halfway down the gangplank, turns around, gets down on one knee and PROPOSES! And she (sort of) said YES!

Can you believe it? My dad and Holly Isles?!

My dad. Perfect Man. (Even if his name doesn't start with a T—Holly says she was just kidding around with me when she said that; "Maybe his first initial is T. Or maybe it isn't," she reckons she said.) Hmmm.

Whatever. Holly keeps telling me how great he is. How smart and kind and wonderful he is. About how she can "be herself" around him, no lessons or plots needed (ouch). About how happy he makes her. About the fact that she feels silly, rushing into yet another relationship, but how, this time, she knows she doesn't have anything to worry about. And if she wasn't talking about my dad, I might be able to stomach it. (Well, so maybe it's a little bit sweet...)

What? Oh, the "pre-" and "sort of" comments. Yeah, I know. I thought you might want me to explain those. I guess they're not really properly engaged. They're kind of like pre-engaged. It's just that Holly wants to take things a bit slower this time. Not rush into anything. But Dad says that's okay, he'll wait for Holly forever. (Every time he tells her this they go revoltingly mushy again and I have to leave the room—really, my stomach's having a tough time of things.)

But anyway, watching him on the gangplank...oh, Alexa, you should have seen it. It was (and I'm sure I'm not allowed to say this, but it was! It really was!): just like a movie.

And you know what? I can't wait for the sequel...

Nessaxxx

ABOUT THE AUTHOR

Allison Rushby lives in Australia, where she has written a whole lot of books. She is crazy about Mini Coopers, Devon Rex cats and corn chips. You can find her at http://www.allisonrushby.com, or procrastinating on Twitter at @Allison_Rushby. That is, when she's not on eBay, or Etsy, or any other place she can shop in secret while looking like she's actually writing...

The SEVEN Month Itch

Living Blond
Book 2

Nessa Joanne Mulholland, aka Marilyn Monroe's No. 1 teenage fan, is living the high life in Manhattan. Literaly. Waffling and pancaking it up every morning (care of housekeeper Vera) in her soon-to-be stepmother's Tribeca penthouse apartment. Things couldn't be better. Or so she thinks, until things start to go terribly, horribly wrong, in true Nessa fashion. All of a sudden, she's starting to feel the need to pull at her collar. Yes, it's summer in NYC and things are heating up fast, including the professor and Holly's wedding plans.

Gasp!

Along with Nessa as her dad's too-gorgeous research assistant moves into the new family penthouse while Holly's away filming in LA...

Cringe!

As Nessa gets dumped for "Doris Day"...

Hiss!

As Kent Sweetman decides he wants Holly back, wedding or no wedding...and

Bite your nails!

As the cupcakiest wedding ever hangs in the balance.

Phew! The temperature's getting hotter by the second, heat rash is setting in fast—and everyone's starting to scratch that Seven Month Itch!

the SEVEN month itch

month itch

Living Blond 2

by

ALLISON RUSHBY

One

"Hey, Vera!" I scramble off my seat at the breakfast bar as soon as I hear the elevator ping.

Even before the doors slide fully open, the heavily accented voice starts in on me. "Hay, it is what the horses eat, *young lady*."

Halfway across the parquetry floor, I stop in my tracks. Young lady? That's a new one. Vera has obviously been spending way too much time hanging around my dad. I shrug, then keep heading in the direction of the very solid form that's now thumping me across the impressively large hallway. "Can I give you a hand?" I go over to take some of the grocery bags Vera's clutching under each arm.

"No, no, no," she clucks in her now-familiar "Me, portly Russian housekeeper; you, child to be overfed" way, and lurches past me into the kitchen. She dumps the bags unceremoniously on the counter with a huff. "Now," she says, turning back around. "What you want for the breakfast?"

Down to Vera business.

I shrug again. "I've already got some juice, and cereal's fine. I was just about to get myself a bowl." I start back the kitchen.

Within seconds, Vera has cut me off at the pass.

"No, no, no," the clucking starts up once more. "You too skinny, Vanessa. So skinny. You need to eat. No cereal. Is all sugar. You need the protein. Too skinny. So skinny!"

I look down at my summer pajama-clad stomach, to see if I've magically lost weight overnight. Nope. And somehow, I don't think that bulge of stomach there is bloating brought on by a severe case of malnutrition.

"See?" she says, and before I can either a) look up, or b) stop her, Vera's pudgy hand has darted out and grabbed my hip-bone. "Nothing!" She gives my hip, and its ample padding, a good squeeze. "Need to eat! Too skinny. So skinny! Boys like the girl with something to hold on to."

Can't argue with that, I guess.

"How about waffles?" I suggest. Never mind the boys, you have to keep your housekeeper happy, right? As Holly's always telling me, it's hard to get good help in Manhattan, especially downtown. Waffles are the least I can do. And if waffles keep the boys interested, well, so be it. We'll call it a welcome side effect.

"Waffles! Yes! Good!" Vera claps her hands together, now a very happy little housekeeper.

"I can help..." I take half a step closer into Vera's kitchen. (When she's here, you have to be very careful about entering. I swear I once heard her start growling when I went to get myself a glass of water.)

"No, no, no. You sit. Drink the juice." And there's the look. The Vera look. The "back away from my kitchen" look.

"Okay," I squeak and turn around to take my seat at the breakfast bar. "I'll just, um, sit here and drink my juice." Who knew that fixing yourself breakfast in your own home could be so dangerous?

"Yes. Good. Drink juice." Then, before I can even take a sip of my juice, the groceries have been put away and scary Vera has turned into happy waffle-making Vera.

I shake my head. If she's anything to go by, Russia must be full of very fat, over-waffled children.

"Morning, Vera! Hey kiddo!" My wicked (in the cool form of the word only) stepmother-to-be breezes into the kitchen.

"Holly, please," I tut. "Hay's what the horses eat." I shoot her a look. "Vera's just been telling me so."

Holly pauses, then laughs. "I wonder who passed that pearl on?"

"Gee, I wonder," I say, rolling my eyes at her. "The professor, perchance?" Ah yes, my dad, Professor William Mulholland, the most embarrassing man in the world. Aside from the usual father–daughter embarrassment, my father couldn't manage to be a professor of something normal, like mathematics or classics, or something. No, my father is a professor of sociology. And his specialty? Human mating rituals. Just my luck.

Holly shakes her head. "Watch it, you. That's my fiancé you're talking about." She chucks me under the chin and laughs again.

Vera looks up from her waffle kingdom. "Ah, so beautiful..." She looks at Holly, sighs, and begins shaking her head sadly. "So beautiful."

"Oh, Vera, cut it out already." Holly waves a hand, blushing.

As for me, I try not to snort my juice out of my nose. This it's-such-a-tragedy-to-be-so-good-looking thing totally cracks me up. I take a look at Holly myself now. The sad thing about it is Vera's right. It really is wrong to be that good-looking before 8 a.m.. All she's wearing is jeans and a white T-shirt, with her long dark hair scraped back into a high ponytail, black sunglasses pushed back on her head, black slides on her feet, a touch of mascara and cherry-tinted lip gloss. She must have taken all of fifteen minutes to get ready, and that includes a shower. Honestly. Couldn't Holly wait till at least 10 a.m. to be beautiful?

"So beautiful..." Vera gives one last sigh before cracking. "Now. What you want for the breakfast? You too skinny! So skinny!"

"Hey!" Marc Harris, Holly's nephew, enters the waffly scene like we're all in some sort of sit-com. I wait for the applause to start...nothing. I guess that's okay as long as it's Marc entering and not me. (He was my one-time dalliance, of course. Then I a) came clean about my age and b) we realized we were going to be kind of related and the ick factor settled in.)

"You too skinny also! Everybody so skinny!"

"Are they waffles?" Marc asks and fearlessly goes right on over to stand next to Vera. He scoops some batter up with his finger. "So good."

Vera nods hard at Marc. "Yes. Good boy!" she says approvingly, before turning back to look at me. "See? He like the waffles."

"Hey! How come you're allowed in the kitchen?" I pipe up now.

Marc gives me a grin. "Because *I* eat like a horse." Another scoop of waffle batter goes in his big mouth.

I sigh, then shrug what I hope is my final shrug of the morning. My shoulders are getting tired already. "Yeah, well, you've got a point. There're only so many waffles a Thoroughbred can take. Unlike old nags headed for the glue factory."

"He growing boy." Vera shakes her ladle at me. "Needs many waffles."

"I thought they were *my* waffles," I protest.

"Now, now, you two. Play nicely." Holly tries on her best mother voice.

"Sorry, Aunty Holly," Marc replies, playing the good nephew. He then turns to face me again, his mouth full of waffle batter. "Hey Nessa, what do you call a smart blonde?"

I groan. Marc hasn't been able to stop with the dumb-blonde jokes ever since he learned a while back that I'm just a tad obsessed with Marilyn Monroe movies. "What?" I ask in reply.

"A golden retriever."

"Ha ha ha."

Holly groans along with me. "When are you going to give up on those dumb-blonde jokes, Marc?"

Um, it's looking like never, I think to myself. As if being blond is funny, anyway. Ha ha. Yes, it's hilarious. And another thing—liking Marilyn Monroe, I mean, what's wrong with that? Who could *not* like her? That's the real question.

Right. I guess I should explain...The thing is, and you might know this, or you might not, but I have a bit of a passion for the big double M. If you do know, sorry, but I'm going to have to explain anyway. I do so love to explain. (My family is always making me do it. I'm practically an expert in the field.) So, why do I have a thing for Marilyn Monroe? Well, because the woman is, was, amazing, of course! I've seen every one of her movies, including the last one that was never finished. And not just once, but about a million times over. Each. I just can't get enough of Marilyn. Why again? Well, I can't exactly explain it. It's not one thing in particular I love about Marilyn, it's just...oh, everything.

"Right. You ready?" I look up to see Holly glance at her watch and then back up at Marc again. "The car will be here any minute."

Marc nods as he licks his fingers. "I'm ready, but my stomach..." At this, he wheels back around to our Russian waffle maker. "Vera..." he asks in what I like to think of as his growing-boy-pleading-with-housekeeper whine. "Can I get those waffles to go?"

"Marc!" Holly gives him a look. "Vera's not your food slave. You can eat something on the plane."

"But Vera's waffles are *so* good and I'm *so* hungry, and plane food is *so* bad and..."I shake my head. Come on, Holly. As if Marc's leaving here without an extra suitcase full of waffles. Vera would rather die first.

Behind me, a breeze blows into the room and I vaguely register that it really feels like summer now. Summer. I can hardly believe it. I zone out as I start to think about what I was doing last summer. It's so weird. This time last year I was living in a tiny one-bedroom apartment with my dad all the way uptown on the Upper West Side. And now, a year later, well, let's just say life is a little different. Now my dad is engaged to Holly Isles. Yes, *the* Holly Isles, one of Hollywood's highest-paid act. And yes, that's *my* dad, the professor. The guy who actually wears those corduroy jackets with patches on the elbows. (If I ever find out where he gets those from, I swear I'll be partaking in a little exercise in arson.)

Sometimes it's hard to get my head around how much has changed in twelve months. Some mornings I still have to pinch myself when I wake up, just to check that it's all for real. I mean, Holly Isles and my dad? It's like Julia Roberts marrying someone like...oh, she married Lyle Lovett, didn't she? Hmmm. Bad example. Okay, then, it's like Catherine Zeta-Jones marrying someone like...oh, bad example again. Well, how about that? Maybe that explains it after all: maybe it's a phase that actors go through.

Still, phase or no phase, there's no denying Holly and my dad's story is pretty romantic. They were from different worlds. He was the geeky professor and she was the stunning. Their eyes met across the crowded deck of the cruise ship where she was honeymooning (without a husband, because her fiancé ditched her at the altar) and he was studying cruise-ship mating rituals. When they parted company in France, it was only to realize they couldn't live without each other. Within months he had chucked in his work in Paris and she'd begged him to move himself and his "people" (that's me) into her Tribeca penthouse. Soon after, she asked him to marry her. (Pretty cool, huh?)

And so, now, here I am.

I turn slightly to look behind me as another breeze blows into the room. Yes. Here I am. In a Tribeca penthouse. Needless to say, it's pretty much nothing like our old apartment on the Upper West Side (unless you stand in the penthouse's hall cupboard, in the dark, where there's a faint musty old-shoe smell, and then it's slightly similar). My eyes practically popped out of their sockets when I realized this was going to be my new home and for the first few weeks, I almost had to resort to taping them in to stop them from popping out ten times a day. Holly calls her penthouse apartment "the Chateau", as a joke. She's told me the story plenty of times. How she went Tribeca apartment shopping (as a girl does on a rainy Saturday) and the real estate agents kept showing her all these boring loft-style warehouse conversions. Then one of the agents took her up to this place, and she said it simply blew her mind.

She's right. It *is* pretty strange. The rest of the building is quite plain, but perched on top, is this miniature castle. Apparently it's "French Provincial" style, whatever that means. I think the best way to describe it is the way I first felt when I stood out on the huge balcony: with its gigantic, intricately carved white plaster pots and curly oversize plaster chairs and benches, the huge oval windows behind looming above me, I swore a gargoyle was going to fly in and carry me away at any moment. Dad says it's like living at Versailles, but in the sky. I wouldn't know, because I've never been to Versailles, but Dad showed me some pictures on the net and I reckon he's pretty close. (I told him maybe next visit to France he won't have us flitting off out of Paris chasing after a woman, and I'll get to see the real thing.) Inside the penthouse, thankfully, there's no guillotine set up in the living room. There're no chandeliers either. The inside is actually quite modern—lots of light blond wood, white furnishings and big gilt mirrors.

So, yes, as I was saying, this summer is shaping up to be...how should I put it? A little different? Just a tad. I take a thoughtful sip of my juice. Still, it's good different. *Really* good different. In fact, I have to say, everything is perfect. Perfect, perfect, perfect. Dad is the happiest he's been in a long, long time. Probably since my mother died. And Holly...well, there's no denying she kind of has this glow when Dad's around (despite him being the most embarrassing guy in the world). It's nice.

I take another sip of juice, smell the waffles cooking in front of me and then pause as my gut gives a twinge. I move in my seat uncomfortably and frown. Nice...perfect...Hmmm. They're words that have been coming up a bit lately. And when they come up that much, I sort of start to worry. You know, worry that things are *too* nice. *Too* perfect. That everyone's *too* happy.

Sometimes I worry that things can't go on like this forever because, the thing is, I can't actually remember being this happy before. Like I said, there was my mother dying then after that, we moved around a lot because of Dad's work at various colleges and universities. It was hard for me to make friends and it was hard for Dad to date.

(One of the reasons we moved so much, I think, was that he wanted an excuse not to date.)

Anyway, now...well, sometimes everything being so "right" all of a sudden seems almost too good to be true. My gut gives another twinge with this thought and I remind myself that I'm not supposed to think like this. I've been through similar patches before where I slightly freak out about things, and so now I pause to remember something a psychiatrist spoke to me about a long time ago, after my mother died. I'd been really worried about my dad dying too, and I'd expected that the psychiatrist, like everyone else, would just tell me that my dad wasn't going anywhere, that he'd be around forever and blah, blah, blah. (And he probably will be, but people telling me that all the time didn't help any. I mean, I thought my mother would be around forever too, right?)

But no, what said was totally different. He told me that nothing is certain in life and that I won't be able to control a lot of things, however hard I try. So, there isn't much use in worrying about what will, or won't, happen tomorrow, or in trying to force things to be one way or another. I just have to ride the wave, enjoy the good times and believe in myself enough to know that I can deal with the bad times that also come my way. I kind of liked him saying that, because it made me feel like I had some control again, like I wasn't just sitting around waiting for more bad things to happen to me.

"Nessa?" Marc's face is in front of mine.

My eyes meet his and still in my where-has-the-past-year-gone? daze, I register that it's going to be weird not having him around after the wedding, once the summer break's over. He's moving right across the country after that, having been accepted into film school in LA. And me? Well, I guess I'll still have Vera. And my waffles. Maybe pancakes tomorrow. Maybe bacon and eggs. Mmm. Yummy. Bacon and eggs and maybe a little hash brown on the side

"NESSA!" Marc's face can't get any closer than this.

"Wha'?" I wake up to myself, still sitting in the same place in the kitchen, waffles before me, and suppress the urge to ask how long I've been out for. Everyone is looking at me. Marc, Holly, Vera and my dad, I notice now, and...oh, who's that? My eyes pause when they meet the new face in the line-up.

"Nessa," my dad speaks up. "As I've already said, er, thrice now, this is Susannah. She's my research assistant for the new project."

I'm not sure what to focus on—the fact that my dad just used the word "thrice" or on Susannah herself. I end up choosing Susannah. "Um, hi," I say.

With her standing right next to Holly, my eyes can't help flitting from one to the other. The contrast almost makes my retinas hurt. Susannah is the exact opposite of tall, dark and curvy old-world Hollywood Holly. She's new-world Hollywood all the way: blond and I think "petite" is the word. (I'd hardly know—no-one has ever used the term to describe me.)

Right. Everyone's really looking at me now. Don't they know it's rude to stare?

And here I am, troll-haired, pajama-ed, on a Monday morning, surrounded by a bevy of beauties—or at least people who have showered—with a towering plate of waffles in front of me. Looking good, Nessa, looking good. But wait. Something's wrong here.

My eyes move swiftly to find Vera now, and I instantly wonder why, when there's a guest in the room, especially such an underfed one, she hasn't tied Susannah down to a chair and started the process of force-feeding (kind of like those geese they force-feed in France so they can make *foie gras* out of their little livers later). But no, there's no force-feeding going on here.

"Hmpf," Vera snorts, giving Susannah the eye. Then she goes back to watching the waffle-maker like a hawk. (It would be a brave waffle that dared to burn on Vera's shift.)

"Yes, well..." My dad looks slightly perturbed at the reaction Susannah's getting here. "It's great that you got to meet Holly," he says, before turning to his fiancée. "Holly, Susannah used to be an actress herself. Before she found sociology, that is."

Holly nods. "Really? That's interesting."

Susannah shakes her head modestly. "Oh, no. You're embarrassing me. I was in a couple of off-Broadway plays. It was nothing."

"Susannah's thesis centers on fame," my dad continues. My ears perk up at this. Fame. Now that *is* interesting. I give her a really good once-over to see how she's reacting to being around Holly.

It's weird, the fame thing. People react in all kinds of different ways when they meet Holly. Some people freak out and tell her they love her, like they've known her forever. Other people pretend they don't know who she is when they obviously do. Once, when we were going to the bathroom at the Time Warner Center, a woman slipped a piece of paper and a pen under Holly's stall and asked for her autograph! It's really rare for someone to act normal the first time they meet Holly. I definitely didn't, that's for sure.

But, to give Susannah credit, she does act pretty normal, and she and Holly end up chatting for a good few minutes about her thesis. Marc, of course, gives his usual "You gotta get through me to get to Holly, lady" glare. He is such a scream. As her nephew, he's lived with the fame thing for a very long time. And while we're all protective of Holly, Marc takes it to another level. When it comes to his aunt, in fact, Marc can be like a yappy little terrier. Watch out for your skinny little ankles, Susannah.

I tune in again to hear Dad still raving on about Susannah's thesis.

"Dumpling, I'm so sorry," Holly cuts him off at the chase, "but I've got to run or we'll miss our plane. I'll call you tonight so you can tell me all about it, okay?"

"Oh, of course," Dad says with a nod.

Holly turns to Susannah. "Now, you've got to promise that you're going to work him hard, Susannah. We've got to have that study proposal finished and submitted before the wedding and the honeymoon." Holly sighs then. "If it wasn't for that stupid

Kent..." And then off she goes on her Kent rant.

We've all heard it a lot lately. Kent Sweetman is her ex-fiancé (real name: Kenneth Mananopolous!) and the reason she and Marc are now headed to LA. Holly thought she'd finished shooting this movie months ago, but now Kent, as co-star and one of the film's producers, has decided he's not happy with a whole heap of scenes and has insisted that they re-shoot them. I think everyone, including Kent, knows he's just doing this to annoy Holly in the lead-up to her wedding, but as a co-producer, he's got the clout to call the shots, even when it comes to Holly Isles.

"Anyway, what was I saying?" Holly interrupts herself. "Oh yes...Work hard, sweet-cheeks." She skips forward to kiss my dad and everyone looks away. (Retch. I mean, I love that they're happy, but my intestines have their limits.)

"And you work hard too, sweet-cheeks the second," Holly says, grinning in my direction.

Oh yeah, I forgot about that. Work. I've got to go there today. Dad got me a part-time job over the summer, working two days a week re-shelving books in the library at the college. I glance at Marc now, standing beside Holly, and wish I hadn't said yes so quickly when Dad first offered. Marc ended up getting the job, going to LA to work as Holly's PA. "I'll try," I tell her as Marc returns my look with a "Have fun, I'm sure I will!" grin.

Like Vera said before, "Hmpf."

"Okay, then. We're off." Holly and Marc head for the elevator.

As they go, Vera presses a huge container of waffles on them, loaded with strawberries, maple syrup and just a dusting of icing sugar. "Here. The waffles. You too skinny! So skinny! Eat! Eat!" Holly laughs. "You're a star, Vera."

Vera pauses. "No. *You* the star," she deadpans.

Holly shakes her head and laughs again. But she also takes the time to crack open the lid of the container and fish out a strawberry. "Mmm. Good!"

"Yes! Eat! Too skinny! So skinny!" Vera keeps right on going, just like the Energizer bunny, even when the elevator doors have closed behind Marc and Holly.

And then, they're gone. Vera turns back to see Susannah right in her path. "Hmpf," she says again and returns to the kitchen.

"Oh! And don't forget..." Everyone whips around at the sound of Holly's voice, as the elevator pings and the doors start to slide open. "Plan me a fabulous wedding, dahling!"

"I will!" I yell back as the doors shut once more. And I can't help but smile as I swivel back around on my seat again.

Get this. Dad and Holly are letting me plan their wedding! They've given me a budget and a basic idea of what they'd like, and are letting me run with it. I keep scaring them by casually leaving brochures for nudist wedding ceremonies and six-foot-tall swan-shaped marshmallow cakes around the apartment. I just can't help myself.

Before I started in on the planning, I thought it would be all fun and cake tasting, but so far it's mostly been plain hard work. In fact, I've spent most of my wedding-planning days doing "fun" things like staggering the post office with a million and one invitation-stuffed envelopes. I don't mind, though. The day itself is going to be amazing. And it's less than two weeks away! I really can't believe it. My dad and Holly Isles. What is my stomach worrying about? I should go with the flow and enjoy this, because everything is simply PPP (perfect, perfect, perfect). Sigh.

Um, er...

Except for the fact that everyone is staring at me again. Well, Dad and Susannah, that is, because Vera, it seems, is busy staring at something else. A suitcase. On the floor. Beside Susannah. It's not Holly's, and it's not Marc's. It's small. Petite. Perfect. PPP...Yes, well, everything was PPP up until about fifteen minutes ago. Because it seems my dad has neglected to tell me a little something about Susannah.

The fact, that is, that she's moving in.

18585796R00078

Printed in Great Britain
by Amazon